Pira
bear
for th

en
w
w.

THE PIRATES!

In an Adventure with Communists

Also by Gideon Defoe

THE PIRATES! IN AN ADVENTURE WITH SCIENTISTS
THE PIRATES! IN AN ADVENTURE WITH AHAB

THE PIRATES!

In an Adventure with Communists

Gideon Defoe

Pantheon Books

NEW YORK

Copyright © 2006 by Gideon Defoe and Richard Murkin
Endpaper map and interior illustrations copyright © 2006 by Dave Senior

All rights reserved. Published in the United States by Pantheon Books, a division of Random House, Inc., New York. Originally published in Great Britain by Weidenfeld & Nicolson, an imprint of the Orion Publishing Group, London.

Pantheon Books and colophon are registered trademarks of Random House, Inc.

Library of Congress Cataloging-in-Publication Data
The Pirates! in an adventure with communists / Gideon Defoe.
p.   cm.
ISBN 0-375-42397-4
1. Pirates—Fiction.   2. Communists—Fiction.   3. Marx, Karl, 1818–1883—Fiction.   4. Nietzsche, Friedrich Wilhelm, 1844–1900—Fiction.   I. Title.
PR6104.E525P568 2006   823.'92—dc22   2006045298

www.pantheonbooks.com

Printed in the United States of America
First American Edition
2 4 6 8 9 7 5 3 1

To Sophie,

who, taking into account the effect of
compound interest, must have even more
than a quarter of a million pounds by now,
so this is her absolute last chance to do right by
me or else I'm dedicating Book Four
to that billionaire Onassis girl,
or maybe the really nice one out of *Lost*.

CONTENTS

One Waggling Weevil
Breakfast – An exciting newspaper story –
Perkins' Pomade – Off to London

Two Tattooed Turtles
In disguise – Getting funny looks –
Buying a nice coat – Under arrest!

Three Thundering Thokes
Languishing in gaol – The criminal mastermind? –
A case of mistaken identity – A business proposition

Four Feckless Flippers
At the rally – A boring lecture – A mysterious blonde –
The Captain agrees to help out

Five Floating Fleets
The difficult guest – A big feast –
A philosophical wager

Six Spliced Shipwrecks
Hard at work – Mutinous swabs! –
The serious thoughts of a pirate captain

Seven Sleepy Starfish
Arriving in Paris – At the Commune – The missing
painting – Waxworks and murder – Dancing girls

Eight Expensive Epaulettes
I'm a cause célèbre! – A mystery gets deeper –
The Captain takes charge

Nine Nautical Nightcaps
A champagne reception – Like a demon! –
Chatting with Wagner

Ten Tangy Tangents
Unmasked! – A countenance like a fish –
Looking for clues

Eleven Equatorial Ensigns
A supernatural fog? – The villain revealed! –
A diabolical plan – Quickly! Through this door!

Twelve Tapered Tabernacles
Live on stage – Up the volcano – A bleak situation –
Philosophy to the rescue

Thirteen Three-square Thermometers
Saying goodbye – Final thoughts

**Appendix – The Wit and Wisdom of the Pirate Captain
– A Major Philosophical Work**

A Note on the Type

One

NIGHTMARE ON
SHARK MOUNTAIN

'The best thing to do,' said the albino pirate, 'is shave his belly with a rusty razor.'

'That's rubbish!' said the pirate with gout. 'You should soak him in a barrel until he grows flippers.'

'You should put him in bed with the Captain's daughter!'

'You should stick a plaster on his back!'

The pirates were sat in the boat's kitchen arguing over what the proper protocol was for dealing with a drunken pirate. After the debate about whether sea anemones made better pretend moustaches or better pretend eyebrows when you stuck them to your face, this was easily the pirates' favourite topic of conversation. Discussions onboard a pirate boat usually escalated into violence without much prompting, and the albino pirate was just about to empty a carton of milk over the pirate with gout's head when the door crashed open and into the kitchen strode the Pirate Captain himself.

Even in slippers and dressing gown, the Pirate Captain cut an imposing figure. If you were to compare him to a type of font – because whilst the pirates usually liked to compare people to types of tree, just recently they had taken to comparing people to other stuff as well, like fonts, or creatures, or makes of cheese – he would undoubtedly be **Impact**, or maybe **Rockwell Extra Bold**. His years of staring at the ocean had given him a nice even tan, and when asked to describe himself in letters to pen friends he would tend to note that he was 'all teeth and curls' but with 'a pleasant, open face'.[1] And most strikingly of all, he wore a great luxuriant beard that the pirates knew had inspired at least one book of epic poetry, because the Captain had personally dictated it on an adventure when it had been too rainy to get up to much else.

'Sorry, Pirate Captain,' said the albino pirate, who knew that they weren't supposed to fight at the breakfast table. 'We didn't mean to disturb you. We were just discussing what the best thing to do with a drunken pirate is. You know how we can never seem to decide.'

---

1. Recent research has shown that people with 'babyish faces' (round face, small nose, large eyes, high forehead and small chin) are seen as less competent as leaders, although presumably more competent at things like crying and eating rusks.

The Pirate Captain looked thoughtful. 'The best thing to do with a drunken pirate,' he said firmly, 'is to give him some strong black coffee.'

And with the argument settled, the Pirate Captain grabbed a tray of breakfast and strode back towards his office.

'He's right,' said the pirate with gout. 'That makes a lot more sense. I don't actually know what "soaking him in a barrel until he grows flippers" even means.'

The Pirate Captain sat back down at the desk in his office, or 'nerve centre' as he had been trying to encourage the men to call it, on account of that sounding more exciting. The cabin was decorated with all kinds of maps, charts, calendars, trophies and at least half a dozen portraits. There was one of the Pirate Captain with a large white whale, the latter smiling weakly and waving its tail. There was a painting of him wearing a string vest and holding a ship's wheel in each hand to draw attention to the musculature in his arms and chest; and another showed him from the rear, walking across a tennis court and scratching his behind. Then there were the gifts from the crew – a series of commemorative plates that depicted famous pirate haircuts, a wind chime made out of miniature cutlasses, a tea towel with '10 Facts About Pirates' and so on. Even the

Captain occasionally got tired of the persistent nautical theme, but he didn't have the heart to tell the men to be a little more imaginative in future. His pirates genuinely loved him, in a manly, shoulder-punching kind of way, and in turn he felt a genuine affection towards his crew. He liked to think of himself as a kind of maritime goatherd, responsible for keeping his pirate goats fed with goat food and warding off wolves and that. The Captain was still working on the metaphor and hoped to share it with them all one day. It had occurred to him to try keeping some actual wolves hidden on the boat and then to set them free to give him an excuse to bring up the whole goatherd-analogy thing, but he wasn't sure where you could get wolves from. He'd certainly never seen any for sale anywhere. The Captain made a mental note: 'Ask number two where I can buy some wolves. Preferably ravening.' Then he went back to reading nautical trivia off the side of his cereal box, because that was where he got most of his seafaring knowledge.

There was a tap at the door, and the pirate with a scarf and Jennifer came in looking excited. Jennifer had been with the pirates for a while now, and she was beginning to blend in. She'd lost some of her characteristic Victorian-lady traits, like wearing corsets that crushed your womb or having hysterical illnesses at the drop of a hat and, eager to be a good pirate, she'd also passed on some of her more charming habits to the crew – it was now a common sight to see pirates brushing their hair a hundred times before bed or self-consciously correcting their posture by walking about with a book on their head.

'Hello, Pirate Captain,' said Jennifer.

'Hello there,' said the Captain. He pointed at his cereal box. 'Did you know that, according to this, pirates wear patches to aid their view of the stars at night? Isn't that something?'

'The world of trivia is amazing,' agreed the pirate with a scarf. 'We've got the morning paper for you.'

'Oh, well, just the cartoon section for me, thanks.'

'I think you should see the front page, sir.'

The Captain glanced up at the paper Jennifer was holding and frowned. '"Communist Dingo Ate My Baby"?'

'Next to that.'

Fishing his glasses out from under a sextant, the Pirate Captain began to read:

DEATH RIDES THE WAVES

The High Seas. In a dramatic battle last night, the Royal Navy's flagship was set upon, ravaged and sunk by a band of ferocious pirates.

EAGLES

Admiral Sedgwick spoke exclusively to this newspaper about his horrific ordeal: 'We were minding our own business, knocking about the ocean, when a huge flotilla of pirate ships sailed out of the fog. They swooped down like eagles in eye patches, waving cutlasses and gnashing their gold teeth.'

SKIN

Though hopelessly outnumbered, our brave Admiral managed to get his officers to safety in a launch. The pirates were led by the ruthless Pirate Captain, who was described by eyewitnesses as all teeth and curls but with a pleasant, open face and devilish flashing eyes. He was accompanied by a cackling pirate wearing a scarf made from human skin. 'When that hellhound gave the order to hole the ship, I looked into his eyes and saw a man without a soul,' reports Admiral Sedgwick. Many fine sailors went to a watery grave.

The Pirate Captain, who is of indeterminate age and no fixed address, apparently took up pirating in a misguided attempt to impress a girl.

'I like the bit about your eyes flashing,' said Jennifer. 'Can you actually make them flash on and off?'

'When the mood takes me,' said the Pirate Captain, looking pleased.

'And is it true about you taking up pirating to impress a girl?'

'Oh, sort of,' said the Captain. 'Truth is, I'm a little tired of telling that anecdote.'

'*Is* that human skin?'

'No,' said the pirate with a scarf. 'It's chinchilla. Nice and warm.'

'Funny thing is,' said the Pirate Captain, knitting his bushy eyebrows together, 'I don't really remember us having an exciting sea battle yesterday.'

'No, Captain,' said the pirate with a scarf, picking a barnacle off the electroplated pirate with an accordion, who was stood in the corner of the office. 'If you recall, we were going to have an exciting battle, but then you got chatting with that admiral and we decided it would be a lot less bother if we just had a competition to see who could eat the most crackers instead.'

'Oh, yes,' said the Captain, brightening. 'That was good. Like at Christmas when the two armies play football with each other.'

'But we were all so engrossed in the cracker contest that nobody was really paying attention to where the boats were going, and the Royal Navy boat ran straight into that iceberg.'

'Aaaarrr. That was unfortunate. Cut through the bow like it was butter, didn't it?'

'Yes, sir.'

'You don't suppose the bow was actually made from butter, though?'

'No, sir. Butter is rarely used in naval construction.'

The Captain shook his head. 'Icebergs. You know, if I didn't already have that fiend Black Bellamy as a nemesis, I think the position could very well be taken by icebergs.'

'They're certainly a nuisance,' said the pirate with a scarf.

'I don't like the way you can't see their eyes,' added the Captain grimly. 'There's something really malevolent about that, don't you think?'

'Um. Icebergs aren't creatures, Pirate Captain.'

'Well, what in the Pirate King's name are they, then?'

'It's when water freezes.'

The Pirate Captain's eyes widened. 'This is what I like about life at sea. It's one long voyage of discovery. Solid water! What will they think of next? Hopefully a pony who solves crimes. Anyhow, you're quite right, I do remember now – we offered them a lift back to port, but he didn't think it would do his reputation much good to be seen with the likes of us. You can see his point. Nice chap that admiral. I like to think that in a different life we might have been friends. Though, of course, in a different life we might both have been moths, or pigs, or something like that. Who's to say?'

'Who indeed, Captain.'

'But if he *had* been a pig and I was a moth, it would be nice to suppose that we could still get along. You know . . . I'd flap my wing at him as I flew past and let him know when he had swill on his nose and so on. Having said that, the bit about me being "a man without a soul" is a little hurtful.'

'I suspect he was probably trying to make things look a bit better to the newspapers than they actually were,' said Jennifer. 'Understandable, really.'

'Aarrrr,' said the Pirate Captain, reading through a bit more of the article. 'I certainly wouldn't want to get on the wrong side of me if that's the kind of behaviour I get up to. Look – at one point I decapitated six sailors with a single swing from my cutlass. And I had the strength "more of a lion than a mortal man".' The Captain made a lion noise.

'But that's not all, sir,' said the pirate with a scarf, looking pleased. 'Because you also got sent this parcel.'

In the Pirate Captain's experience parcels had been a bit of a mixed blessing. He'd had good things come in parcels, like a nice T-shirt from Coney Island, a stuffed crow and a mug of hot tea, but he'd also had some bad things, like a pile of mouldy potatoes, a hideous porcelain horse and a gauntlet that had turned out to be haunted. Luckily, this was definitely one of the good kind of parcel because it contained a letter, some tins of hair pomade and a small chest of treasure.

9

'Why are people sending us treasure, Captain?' asked Jennifer, opening up the chest.

'It's from the good people at Perkins' Gentlemen's Pomade,'[2] explained the Pirate Captain, waving the letter at them. 'It seems that due to my new-found fame and notoriety they're proposing to sponsor our adventures. All I have to do is occasionally mention what a fine product they produce and how I couldn't live a day without it, that kind of thing, and in return they'll send us a monthly stipend, in the form of jewels and gold doubloons and that.'

Perkins' Gentlemen's Pomade
Makes your hair look quite nice,
Have shiny flowing locks,
At an affordable price!

'Oh, that *is* nice,' said the pirate with a scarf. 'There are too few heart-warming moments at sea.'

---

2. Bear grease became popular as a pomade after a tax was imposed in 1845 on hair powder. It was common for barbers to display a dead bear on their premises and advertise that it had been 'freshly killed today!'.

Jennifer tried on a tiara from the chest. It suited her. 'What are you going to spend it on, Captain?'

'How about some new sails?' said the pirate with a scarf, practical as ever. He tried on a different tiara, but the emeralds clashed with his scarf. 'Or portholes that don't let the water in; that would be nice.'

'I think we have to prioritise, number two,' said the Captain gravely. 'It's all very well wanting luxuries like new sails or portholes with glass in them, but there are also much more pressing necessities. Like me getting a nice new coat.'

'You only got that coat last week, Captain!' said Jennifer with a frown. 'For that pirate conclave in Nassau. I remember because Cut-throat Jenkins had exactly the same design. It was something of a social faux pas.'

'Ah, but you see, it's ruined. Probably in last night's exciting sea battle,' said the Pirate Captain. He held up the hem of his coat, where a tiny piece of stitching had come loose.

'It's only a small tear,' said the pirate with a scarf. 'I can mend that in no time. Remember that adventure where we set up a Bond Street fashion house and Black Bellamy had a rival fashion house and we competed in London Fashion Week?'

'The one where my daring take on traditional tailoring took the fashion world by storm and Black Bellamy cheated by copying the exact same designs and managed to get them on to the catwalk just before we did?'

'Yes, that's the one. Anyway, I picked up quite a few sewing skills.'

'That's good of you, but I think this damage is beyond repair, number two.' The Pirate Captain grabbed the bottom of his coat and tore it another foot and a half. 'See? That could happen at any time. I definitely need a new one. So we'll stop off in London, give the lads some shore leave and get me a new coat. Don't worry, after that we'll have some sort of adventure – hopefully something light involving a heist or a missing dinosaur skeleton. Or perhaps something to do with a barnyard. Have we ever had an adventure in a barnyard?'

'I don't think so, sir,' said the pirate with a scarf.

Two

BLONDE CAPTIVE OF THE CLAMS

The pirates left the boat in the Thames, next to the Palace of Westminster. They deliberately parked across two disabled spaces, because that kind of behaviour was pretty much the whole point of being a pirate. Back in those days the Thames wasn't the beautiful crystal-blue colour it is today, and it didn't have children splashing playfully about on its sandy banks. It was grey and drab and had old shopping carts floating in it. And you couldn't cup your hands in the river and drink its delicious water like you can now, on account of all the pollution. Pollution came from the factories, because the factories of Victorian times didn't make iPods and Internets and shiny DVDs – they made large clouds of black smoke, which were sold to countries that didn't have so much in the way of clouds, like Africa.[3]

The first thing the Pirate Captain did was make sure everybody was wearing their disguises. Several of the pirates had been hoping that the disguise would be squid, because they enjoyed playing about with the tentacles and slapping each other in the face with the suckers; but the Pirate Captain, keen to try something new, decided that the best disguise would be a party of schoolchildren visiting from France. He himself would take the role of a harmless French schoolmaster.

'Because acting like children plays to your strengths,' the Captain pointed out. 'Be sure to wear your outsized backpacks, and bump into as many angry Londoners as possible with them.'

'Aren't we a little old to be schoolchildren?' asked the pirate in red.

The Pirate Captain surveyed his crew and had to admit to himself that the pirate in red had a point. The pirates weren't quite as fresh-faced and rosy-cheeked as they'd once been. Some of them had even begun growing tufty little beards in a flattering, if hopeless, attempt to emulate their captain.

'Well then. You can pretend to be slightly retarded schoolchildren who have been held back a few years.

---

3. During the 'Great Stink' of 1858 pollution in the Thames became so bad that the Houses of Parliament had to be abandoned.

This had the added advantage of making me look like a caring sort in front of any women we happen to meet on this adventure.'

'Do you actually know any French, Pirate Captain?' asked the pirate with a nut allergy.

'I'm fluent, thank you. Almost like a native,' said the Captain, with a scowl. The Pirate Captain knew the French for 'This is a pretty donkey' and also 'This is not a pretty donkey', and he couldn't think of anything that wasn't either a pretty donkey or not a pretty donkey, so that was just about every eventuality covered.[4]

'Go on then. Say something in French.'

'I'm not a performing monkey,' said the Captain testily. 'Though I'd probably be a lot better off if I was. A monkey who could speak French. I'd be touring Europe with a talent like that, not hanging about with swabs like you.'

The pirates went on looking at him expectantly.

'Oh, all right. *C'est un joli donkey.*'

'Is that supposed to be a French accent? It sounds more like a sort of Welsh Geordie,' said the pirate in red.

'How is it you're even here? Didn't we leave you inside a whale on our last adventure?'

---

4. One of the most fundamental principles of logic is:

If p = true → ~ p = false

In other words, if I have eaten your side of beef, I can't not have eaten your side of beef. It may sound obvious, but a lot of people cleverer than us have spent years sorting this sort of thing out.

The pirate in red shrugged. 'Oh, you know. I guess I must have gotten out at some unspecified point.'[5]

And so the pirates, walking in an orderly crocodile formation, made their way through the grime-covered streets towards the Pirate Captain's favourite Savile Row tailors. There was so much mud about the place that the albino pirate said he wouldn't be surprised if a dinosaur came walking over the brow of Holborn Hill, but the rest of the pirates told him off for saying stupid things like that. The Captain was a bit fed up to see that there still weren't any blue plaques dotted around to mark out important moments in his youth, such as the butcher's where he used to press his nose against the glass and gaze adoringly at the hams when he was a little boy, or the alleyway round the back of Covent Garden where he had first kissed a girl with tongues. He resolved to step up his letter-writing campaign to the mayor.

The pirates hadn't got very far before it became obvious something was amiss. Even though the Pirate Captain was doing his best to exude a friendly Gallic charm, everywhere they walked, people seemed to be pointing at him. The pirates had always been told it was rude to

---

5. Many of the best novels have glaring plot inconsistencies. In Daniel Defoe's Moll Flanders, Moll marries her older brother, who was somehow born several years later than she was.

point, so they were a bit shocked by this. A few of the more grimy onlookers grinned and waved, but most of the people shook their fists and cursed, or grabbed their children and drew back inside their houses in fright.

'You're getting a lot of funny looks, Captain,' said the pirate with a scarf. 'I mean, more so than usual.'

'From well-to-do types? Yes, I've been noticing that. I suspect they're probably jealous of my free and easy lifestyle.'

'It looks like our brilliant disguises aren't working so well.'

'Aaarrr. Which is odd, because normally, as you well know, I come up with disguises that are frankly foolproof. Perhaps I'm losing my touch.'

The Pirate Captain found himself experiencing mixed moods, which didn't really agree with him. On the one hand he was a little annoyed that people seemed to be seeing through his disguise so easily, but on the other hand he was pleased that his diabolical reputation had obviously spread so far so quickly. He was just about to tell the pirate with a scarf that with this sort of notoriety perhaps they should have held out for a little more from the Perkins' Gentlemen's Pomade people, when he turned a corner and found himself smacked upside the head by a handbag.

'You're a terrible, *terrible* man!' said the old lady whose handbag it was. She glowered, gave him another smack for good measure and then hobbled off down the street.

'I'm not sure that was entirely called for,' said the Pirate Captain, a little dazed, gingerly rubbing his face.

'You're going to have a shiner there,' said the pirate with a scarf. He sighed, and resigned himself to being up all night rubbing the Captain's belly for him. Most people don't get stomach ache from being smacked in the face, but whenever the Pirate Captain ended up with a black eye – something that happened a surprising amount on his adventures – the pirate with a scarf would insist on putting an uncooked steak on it to bring down the swelling. And every single time, the Captain would solemnly promise that he wouldn't eat the raw steak, and usually not more than an hour later the pirate with a scarf would notice that the steak had vanished, and he would ask the Captain what had happened to the steak and the Captain would say that a coyote had made off with it but that the coyote had been moving so fast he wasn't surprised the pirate with a scarf hadn't seen it. And about an hour after that the Pirate Captain would start complaining of belly pains.

This time, before the Pirate Captain could make any meat-related promises, there was a tug on his sleeve, and he looked down to see a sooty street urchin.

'My dad thinks you're a great man,' said the urchin. 'He says it's fantastic what you're trying to do for us chimney sweeps.'

The Pirate Captain couldn't really remember ever trying to do anything in regard to chimney sweeps, except dislodge them from the boat's chimney when they died and got stuck up there. But he grinned anyway.[6]

'Well, you know, one does one's best. I don't do autographs, I'm afraid, in case you turn out to be Black Bellamy disguised as a fan, getting me to unwittingly sign a cheque for a thousand pounds. Not going to get caught with that one again. But I do have these badges.' The Pirate Captain rummaged in his pocket and brought out a three-colour badge that said 'I like the Pirate Captain and his adventures!'

The sooty urchin took the badge, looked a bit confused and bounded off.

'Little scamp. Probably off to steal pies from a window sill, or snort glue out of a paper bag. Makes me nostalgic for my youth,' said the Pirate Captain.

'This is all getting very strange,' said the pirate with a scarf, pulling a thoughtful face.

The Pirate Captain sighed. 'You realise the problem of course? No disguise can hide my natural nautical charm.'

'*Possibly* that's it,' said the pirate with a scarf, sounding a bit uncertain.

---

6. To make chimney sweeps work faster, people in Victorian times used to start a fire whilst they were still inside the chimney, hence the expression 'lighting a fire under you'. Also, it is considered lucky for a woman to be kissed by a chimney sweep on her wedding day, though chimney sweeps may have made this up as an excuse to get off with girls.

'The only *really* strange thing is that I've been in the pirating business as long as I have and it's only now I'm being afforded the recognition I deserve. But don't worry, I'm not going to let fame change me. I'll still be the humble, modest figure you've all grown to love. Except maybe with a nice silver-topped cane. And I might start demanding that from now on you wash my beard only in the tears of a newborn lamb. Actually, make a note of that one, number two.'

The pirate with a scarf dutifully wrote down 'Lamb's tears' in his notebook.

'Right, here we are,' said the Pirate Captain, coming to a halt in front of a small shop with an understated skull-and-crossbones sign hanging above the entrance. 'I shouldn't be too long. You lot can go and sit about in coffee shops winking at waitresses or whatever it is you do during shore leave. I'll see you in about an hour.'

The shop bell jingled a rough approximation of a popular shanty as the Pirate Captain opened the door. 'Willoughby and Sons' had been the pirate gentlemen's outfitter of choice for over three centuries. The Pirate Captain had heard that before Willoughby's opened, pirates would wear anything that came to hand, such as big leaves, old bits of sacking or even dungarees. But thankfully, the modern pirate captain's reputation relied as much on the cut of his clothes as his ability to get treasure, romance governors' daughters or practise some sort of reign of terror over the oceans.[7] He closed the door behind him and happily inhaled the rich scent of mothballs and starfish.

The tailor was dealing with another customer, so the Captain decided to browse. He ran his finger along rows of brightly striped britches and blousy shirts, before examining a display of immaculately folded eye patches. He was particularly keen on one with a big pretend eye stitched over where your real eye would be. The Pirate Captain had always thought he'd look good with one eye bigger than the other. As he tried, in vain, to fold the eye patch back up, he felt a light touch on his arm and heard a discreet cough.

'Could I help you, sir?' asked the tailor. He was a neat little man, with a bright-pink face and every single grey hair plastered precisely into place. The Pirate Captain suspected he used varnish to make it so shiny. Realising who his customer was, the tailor beamed. 'Pirate Captain! So good to see you! And such a disguise! Let me guess now . . . You are meant to be some sort of squid, yes?'

The Pirate Captain held up his exercise book and

---

7. If a pirate were to walk down the street nowadays, he'd probably be wearing tight drainpipe jeans and a form-fitting T-shirt. Baggy clothing was not practical on a ship, where it could get in the way when climbing the rigging.

piece of chalk. 'French schoolteacher. Not one of my best, to be honest.'

'No, no, I see it now. A French schoolteacher. Very good. Don't forget that we now carry a small range of disguises for the gentleman pirate. Our "pensioners' day out" is particularly popular at the moment.'

He started to bustle about with his tape measure, sizing up the Pirate Captain.

'Now, I think for a man of your fearsome reputation, you'll be wanting a pair of imposing boots. Am I right? No offence intended to your current footwear, sir, but many of my customers have adopted this season's hand-stitched pirate boots, designed specifically for stomping about and creating an ungodly racket that terrifies the lubbers.'

'Actually, I'm after a new coat. Owing to the pressures of fame, I'm in a bit of a hurry, so it will have to be off the peg rather than bespoke.'

The tailor suppressed a shudder. 'Off the peg,' he said. 'Of course. Have I ever told you what an uncommonly broad neck you have, Pirate Captain?'

'You have, but feel free to mention it again.'

'Like a bull. I don't think I've ever seen the like before.'

'You're right,' said the Captain, looking approvingly at himself in a full-length mirror. 'I should try to come up with a way of dropping that into conversation more often.'

'What sort of coat would sir be wanting?'

'Something tasteful. Lots of epaulettes. Complicated frogging all down the front. And gold braid. Yards and yards of gold braid. It's like my Aunt Joan used to say – can't ever have too much gold braid. Do you have anything like that in stock?'

The tailor riffled through a rack of pirate coats.

'This is a popular design, Pirate Captain. It depicts action scenes from the Norse myths, picked out in red and green stitching, so that if viewed using special spectacles the whole design appears to be three-dimensional.'

'That must scare the wits out of everybody. Sounds like just the thing.' The Captain pulled on the coat and tried out a few nautical poses. 'Though how do you get your victims to wear the spectacles?'

'We've found that it helps if you tell them that they will be able to see through women's clothes.'

'Well, I'm sold. Chuck in a couple of pairs of the glasses, will you?'

'A great choice, Pirate Captain, if I can be so bold. Thanks to Mr Wagner's operas, this style is all the rage at the moment. The West End is abuzz with Viking mania, I'm told.'

'Hum. Not really my kind of thing, operas,' said the Pirate Captain thoughtfully. 'All that singing-for-nine-hours-without-a-break nonsense. I might have the neck of a bull, but between you and me, I have the bladder of a tiny child.'

'Nothing to be ashamed of, sir. Regular urination is vital for healthy digestion.'

'Exactly what I always say. It so happens I killed a whale on our previous adventure by blocking its blow-hole and thus preventing it from expelling whale wee. And they say that we're only one step up from fishes, in evolutionary terms. So no opera for me – I don't fancy exploding.'

'You're right, of course, Captain. But I must say I have a certain yen for those big-boned, statuesque blonde operatic ladies.'

'Really? I'm more of a "gazelle-like legs and delicate shoulders" kind of man. Meaning sleek like a gazelle, not with a backward-facing knee. That would be horrible.'

'It's just my opinion,' said the tailor, looking a bit wistful, 'but you can't beat the powerful Nordic frame. I like a lady who looks like she spends most of her time knocking about fjords, having competitions to see how far she can throw a penguin.'

'Well, each to their own.'

The shop bell tinkled again, and two mutton-chopped Victorian gentlemen walked in furtively. One of them pointed at the Pirate Captain. The Pirate Captain rolled his eyes.

'This is the trouble with celebrity: never a moment to yourself. Sorry about this. Can't disappoint my public.' He turned to face the two men.

'Hello there. Yes. You're right, it *is* me. I suppose you

want a photograph? Don't bother with the "it's for my wife" rigmarole when really it's for you but you're ashamed to admit that you hero-worship another man. It's quite all right in this day and age.'

One of the mutton-chopped men reached forward, the Pirate Captain assumed to shake his hand. Since learning of his notoriety, he had been practising a new handshake. It started firm and confident before shifting to a kind of pumping movement that he felt conveyed both 'steely resolve' and 'compassionate man of the people.' The Captain grasped the gent's hand and got going, but was rather surprised when the fellow pulled out a set of handcuffs and snapped them shut on his hairy wrist.

'You're under arrest!' said the mutton-chopped man.

And then for the second time that afternoon the Pirate Captain found himself getting smacked about the head, though this time it was with a truncheon, which was a lot more effective than a handbag. He was just wondering whether pork chops would be as good as steaks for bringing down swelling or whether it was something particular about beef that did the trick, when a second blow knocked him out cold.[8]

---

8. As the steak deteriorates it releases 'protease', which helps break down clots and speeds up the healing process.

Three

I SAW SEA
CUCUMBERS EAT
JENKINS!

The Pirate Captain sat on a bare wooden bunk in a police cell. Through the single small window, he watched a tired-looking monkey pull a rotating triangular sign that said 'Scotland Yard' around and around outside. Annoyingly, no tiny bird landed on the window sill, because if one had, the Captain had a great speech worked out about how the bird should fly away and be free, whilst he languished there for ever. How long, he wondered, had he already been held like this? Days? Weeks? Months? He looked at his fingernails to see if their length gave him any clue.[9] Then he remembered

---

9. Nails grow at an average of 0.1 mm per day. This rate varies according to a number of factors including age, season, fitness and genetics, so it is actually a rubbish way of telling the time.

that his pocket watch was probably a bit more accurate than fingernails, so he looked at that instead. He was a little disappointed to see that so far it had only been fifteen minutes. Just as he was about to make a start on some sort of sad ballad, the gaol door swung open and in walked a policeman.

'About time!' exclaimed the Pirate Captain, leaping to his feet and pulling an indignant face. 'Honestly, I'm appalled. Treating a harmless French schoolteacher like this. It could cause a diplomatic incident between our two countries. We might cut off your supply of fancy French sauces. Then where will you be?'

The policeman sat down opposite him and fixed him with a serious stare.

'*Les jeux sont faits,*' he said.

'Pardon?'

'Translation: the game is up!'

'Oh, right, yes. I knew that, because I'm French.' The Pirate Captain pointed at the table. '*Ce n'est pas un joli donkey.*'

'It's no use, you villain. We know exactly who you are,' said the policeman, waggling a thick pile of papers at the Captain. 'Whilst your perfect French is obviously impressive, it's no more than we'd expect from a criminal mastermind.'

'Oh, really? Bother.' The Captain slumped back in his chair, shook his head sadly and not for the first time wondered what on earth had made him choose piracy over architecture. 'I suppose I knew this day was coming. In some ways it's even a relief. But in other, much more fundamental, ways it's very annoying.' He sighed and ran his fingers through his beard. 'Well, it goes without saying that I'd be especially willing to turn king's witness and testify against Black Bellamy. And I'd like to point out that all my crimes were in self-defence anyway. Even that time we attacked all those women and children. Or the lepers. They can be surprisingly vicious, you know.'

The Pirate Captain found himself thinking back to an earlier adventure with Freemasons, and a little plan formed in his piratical brain.

'Goodness me, a bit hot in here, isn't it? Don't mind if I loosen these clothes a little?' he said, pulling open his coat and starting to unbutton his shirt. 'Oh look, there's my nipple,' he added, licking his finger, winking conspiratorially at the policeman and rubbing his hairy chest a bit for good measure. The policeman just frowned, and the Pirate Captain suddenly remembered that he might have been confusing his adventure with Freemasons with his adventure with pole dancers. He sheepishly did his shirt back up.

'If you've quite finished,' said the policeman, starting to read from a list in front of him. 'You're to be charged with numerous breaches of the peace—'

'Ah, now,' the Pirate Captain cut in quickly. 'That probably wasn't me. I bet it was Gary, our ship's parrot.

We got him from a creature sanctuary, you see, and whoever his last owner was seems to have taught him all sorts of terrible words that you'd never hear me use. And he does tend to shout them out at inopportune moments. Possibly he has an avian version of that Tourette's syndrome. Can parrots get that?'[10]

The policeman didn't seem to be listening. '... Then there's activities that seek to shake the economic foundations of Great Britain and her Empire ...'

'Shaking the economic foundations of the country? Are you sure? It's just stealing a few necklaces and jewels and that. And, if I'm being honest, we're not even a particularly successful outfit. Most of the time we just end up with some nice-looking shells if we're lucky. Is the economy really that fragile?'

'... and further activities that seek to encourage unrest amongst the populace.'

'You mean the way my glamorous piratical lifestyle makes regular folk question the direction of their humdrum lives? I don't think I can really be blamed for that. Though I suppose I could try to tone down my raw sexuality.'

'Do you have anything sensible to say for yourself?' asked the policeman, folding his arms.

'I certainly do,' said the Pirate Captain, leaning forward.

---

10. A 105-year-old parrot called Charlie entertains visitors to a Surrey shopping centre with obscene anti-Nazi tirades. Claims that the parrot was once owned by Winston Churchill have not yet been verified.

'Is it true you keep your sandwiches under your hats? I've always wanted to know that.'

Before the policeman had a chance to reply, there was a scuffling sound from outside and then the door flew open and in bowled a serious-looking young man with a shock of blond hair.

'This is an outrage, you brutes! This gentleman,' he said, pointing at the Pirate Captain, 'is both a respected philosopher and a pillar of the community!'

The Pirate Captain winced. He could just imagine what the Pirate King would say if word got back that he was being described in terms like 'pillar of the community' instead of 'black-hearted and briny master of the waves'.[11]

'I wouldn't go that far,' he said, feeling that he had to set the record straight. 'I mean, I really am mischievous and roguish. I hardly ever pay taxes. And I don't think a day goes by when I eat the recommended five portions of fruit and vegetables. Would a pillar of the community set that kind of example for the kids?'

The young man looked at the Pirate Captain. He did a double take. Then he frowned. 'You're not Dr Marx!' he exclaimed.

'Dr Marx? No,' the Captain agreed. 'I did nurse a puppy back to health that one time. But I don't hold any

---

11. In cooking, brining is the practice of soaking meat in salt water prior to cooking. Brined meat is more moist when served, due to denatured proteins forming a matrix that traps water molecules.

formal medical training. Assuming you mean that kind of a doctor. If you mean the academic kind of doctor, I'm not that either, owing to some issues concerning unpaid library fines, which I'd rather not go into. And my name isn't Marx. Actually, my name is a mystery that I've sworn not to reveal until my final adventure. So you're right on both counts. I'm assuming you're not Dr Marx either?'

The young man turned back to the policeman and glowered. 'I'd been told you'd arrested Karl Marx.'

'Yes, we have. That's to say, haven't we?' The policeman looked confused.

'No, sir, you have not. Dr Marx does not avail himself of fripperies like gold-trimmed coats.'

'It's a tasteful Viking theme,' said the Pirate Captain. 'See, if I bump my arms together, it looks like Thor is fighting Odin. Or kissing him, depending on your mood.'

'Also, Dr Marx does not normally sport an eye patch. I think you'll find somebody has just disrespectfully doodled that on to your "wanted" poster. And whilst in many ways this man bears an uncanny resemblance to Marx, the good doctor doesn't smell so much of the salty ocean. And he has a beard of even greater extent and luxuriousness.'

'Steady on,' said the Pirate Captain.

There followed a great deal of squinting at the "wanted" poster and then squinting at the Pirate

Captain. The policeman tried to argue that if you shut one eye and turned your head on its side then you almost had a match, but eventually he had to admit that the young man with the blond hair was right and that the Pirate Captain really wasn't the notorious Karl Marx, though it was an understandable mistake to make, especially in an era before electricity and proper lights.

'Sorry. We're always having these sorts of mix-ups,' said the policeman, handing the Captain his hat and cutlass back. 'The other day we thought we'd cornered a dangerous international terrorist, but it turned out to be a pillar box that somebody had forgetfully left their hat on top of. The envelope slot looks a bit like a mouth.'

'So I'm free to go?' said the Pirate Captain, feeling a little aggrieved despite himself. 'What about all the living above the law and terrorising the shipping lanes business? I still do all that,' he added with a pout.

'Nautical matters,' replied the policeman with a shrug. 'That's outside our jurisdiction, I'm afraid.'

'What if I stole the Crown jewels but then used my boat to escape?' the Captain suggested.

'I suppose that might count. You're not planning on doing that, are you?' asked the policeman, looking a bit anxious.

'Not really, no. Still, it's good to check these things in advance, just in case the situation crops up.'

The blond man and the Pirate Captain stood outside the police station, waiting for the rain to pass.

'I'm the Pirate Captain,' said the Pirate Captain, trying to be friendly.

'Friedrich Engels,' said the blond man, shaking the Captain's hand.

'Thanks for helping sort out the mix-up, though obviously I had a clever plan of escape worked out anyway. It would have involved building a replica of myself out of old vegetable scraps.'

'My pleasure,' said Engels, lighting a cigarette nervously. He looked again at the Captain and shook his head in wonder. 'You really are quite his spitting image.'

'Humph,' said the Pirate Captain. 'You're honestly trying to tell me this Marx fellow has a beard to rival mine? You're sure it wasn't just the bad light in there? Now we're outside, take a proper look at it. Do you see the way the daylight brings out the russet hues around the edges?'

'No, you're right, it's not quite the same. I feel Dr Marx's beard is perhaps that little bit more voluminous.'

The Pirate Captain snorted indignantly. 'I find that a little difficult to believe.'

'Sorry,' said Engels. 'I didn't mean to offend.'

There was an awkward silence. A hansom cab clattered by. Somewhere, a rat squeaked.

'Ooohh . . . *rain*,' said the Pirate Captain after a few moments. He rolled his eyes to emphasise the point.

'Wait a moment!' exclaimed Engels. 'Are you the pirate captain who was all over the newspapers the other day? It mentioned that he rolled his eyes "like the furies of Hell were snapping at his heels".'

'Yes, that's me. But you know the newspapers, they exaggerate such a lot. Really I only decapitated five sailors with that cutlass stroke.'

Engels paused, looked furtively about and then pulled a leaflet from his pocket. He pressed it into the Captain's hand. 'Dr Marx is giving a talk tonight. I'd very much like you to come along. Listen, Pirate Captain, I may have . . . a business proposition for you.'

And with that, and a brisk nod of his head, Engels disappeared down the alleyway.

The Pirate Captain found the rest of the pirates shopping in Harrods. They were having a heated conversation with an exasperated clerk.

'What about a puppy, but instead of a puppy's head, with the head of an alligator?' said the albino pirate.

'No. We've not got that,' said the clerk.

'How about a zombie eagle?'

'No. We've not got that either.'

The pirates saw their captain and waved.

'This is rubbish, Pirate Captain,' said the pirate in green. 'It says on the door that Harrods sells anything, but so far they haven't had a single item we've asked for.'

'Just buy a packet of crisps so we get a Harrods bag,' said the Pirate Captain sensibly, 'and then we'll grab a coffee and you can hear the harrowing tale of mistaken identity and police brutality I have to tell. Though I should warn you in advance, it's not for the faint-hearted.'

Soon the Pirate Captain was strolling through Hyde Park telling his crew all about life on the inside.[12]

'You have to survive on your wits, really. Especially a good-looking fellow like myself. There was a real risk I could have been traded around by my cell mate for a packet of cigarettes. And it's important not to drop the soap. Though having said that, I'll miss the camaraderie. Taking new prisoners under your wing, showing them the ropes, that kind of thing.'

'We're very glad you're free again,' said the pirate with a scarf.

'Yes. Freedom. Difficult to adjust to that.' The Captain

---

12. Hyde Park was laid out by the architect Decimus Burton, which is a brilliant name. He also designed the llama building at London Zoo.

furrowed his brow and did his best thousand-yard stare. 'I hope I haven't become institutionalised.'

'I think it takes longer than half an hour to become institutionalised, Pirate Captain.'

'You can be very harsh at times, number two. Anyhow, obviously ninety per cent of this attention we've been getting is as a result of my genuine and undoubted piratical fame. But it does appear that *some* of it may be a result of people mistaking me for this Karl Marx fellow.'

The pirates all made reassuringly disbelieving 'as if' noises.

'It says here that he's a communist,' said the Captain, reading from the flyer, 'which I'm fairly sure is a circus thing, isn't it? This Engels man, who seems to be the sidekick, invited us to hear him speak tonight. He mentioned a business proposition, which tends to mean they want me to sign something or press the flesh with potential clients. Endorse the show and so on.'

'Oh, bother. I thought we could go to the opera,' said the pirate with long legs. 'I'm told this Wagner thing is brilliant.'

'I'd rather stay on the boat and knock nails into my head,' said the Pirate Captain sternly.

He paused to watch some children sailing toy boats on the lake. Then he kicked at a stone and gave a little cheer when it hit and sank one of them.

'I know that seemed a little harsh,' the Captain said,

catching the looks some of his men were giving him, 'but think of it as maintaining my image. In today's fickle media climate I can't risk becoming yesterday's notorious buccaneer. There are thousands of aspiring pirate captains out there.'

'Like this Dr Marx?' asked the pirate in green.

'Do you know, that must be it! He's probably trying to take my place as public enemy number one by copying my look and sticking up posters of himself everywhere. It's sad, really, to have to stoop to those sorts of levels. So let's find out what he has to say for himself.' The Captain did the flashing thing with his eyes again. 'Besides everything else, I'm keen to see if this so-called beard of his is all it's cracked up to be.'

Four

DEATH CAN BE SQUID-SHAPED

Soho wasn't the most salubrious part of Victorian London, but what it lacked in top-hatted gentlemen and women in crinolines it more than made up for with cholera, hollow-eyed beggars and plenty of infant death. As they made their way towards the pub where Marx was holding his talk, the pirates were especially touched to hear so many of the ladies who were slouched in doorways ask if they were looking for a good time, which the Pirate Captain explained was down to a natural chirpy cockney friendliness. Eventually, they came upon a small queue of earnest-looking communists waving placards.

'Very nice,' said the pirate in green, trying to be polite. 'I like the blood dripping from that dollar sign.'

'Are you particularly into hammers and sickles, then?' said the albino pirate, looking at the little flag pinned up above the entrance to the pub.

'Oh, you know. All sorts of tools,' said a communist. 'It's kind of our logo.'

'Really? I'm sure you could do better than that,' said the pirate in red. 'The best logos tend to have skulls in them. Or how about some sort of anthropomorphic talking animal? They're always popular. "Sparky the communist firefly" – something along those lines?'

At the front of the queue, a man with a long, brown beard was doing his best to look furtive. 'You cannot enter without a password,' he said, holding up a hand and sounding stern.

'Oh, right. This is fun! How many guesses do I get?' said the Pirate Captain, doing his most conspiratorial face.

'You get three.'

'Is it "brine"? That's a good password. It's actually just salt water, but it sounds more enigmatic. Brine. Say it with a Scottish accent – that's even more mysterious.'

'It's not "brine".'

'Hmmm . . . Is it "barnacle"?'

'No. One guess left!'

'"Barnacle" would be an excellent password. I'd say barnacles are the most mysterious fish in the whole sea. Nobody knows what they are. I've always thought they might be little eyes, but some of the men think they're actually the ghosts of dead sailors. A bit far-fetched for me. What do you think?'[13]

'I'm afraid I have no idea.'

'Oh well, it was worth a try. Anyway, the password is "hello". I was just mucking about with you, because it's actually written on the back of your hand there, isn't it?'

The inside of the pub was dark and smoky, and its walls were covered in slightly moth-eaten stuffed animals and

---

13. Catholics used to argue that the barnacle goose, Branta leucopsis, came from barnacles rather than eggs, because this meant they would be classified as fish instead of birds and so could be eaten during Lent.

paintings of singing cats. The Pirate Captain winced a bit as he recalled an unsuccessful adventure where he'd taken up taxidermy to make the pirates individual stuffed Christmas presents. It had turned out that taxidermy was rather more technical than he'd expected, and to this day he'd never quite got the smell of bird innards out of some of the crew.

They made their way upstairs and jostled to find seats. The place was already full to bursting, and they had to push past quite a few grumbling communists who didn't seem to welcome French schoolchildren. Engels emerged from a door at the back of the room and stepped up to the podium. He motioned for quiet.

'Hello, comrades,' said Engels.

'Hello, Engels,' replied the communists.

'Any capitalist spies in tonight?'

A few men with stuck-on beards waved.

'Would you mind leaving?' asked Engels politely. 'We've nothing to hide, it's just that there aren't enough chairs and some real communists are having to stand at the back. Thanks.'

The spies left cheerfully, and Engels pressed on.

'Now, I know you're all eager to hear Dr Marx speak, but this is a party meeting and I'm afraid I have to denounce a few comrades first. So . . . the following have behaved contrary to the interests of the international proletariat and are no longer considered party members: Tamsin Virgo, parlourmaid – expelled for wearing reactionary hats. Robert Adey, cabinetmaker – expelled for laughing at a postcard that Dr Marx has deemed to be inappropriately pro-bourgeois. And finally Fiona Hankey, dressmaker – expelled for not pulling her weight in the tea-making sphere.'

The denounced communists stood and trudged miserably out of the room, while the rest of the audience tutted loudly to show their disapproval of such backsliders. Engels waited patiently and resumed in a slightly deeper, more portentous voice.

'Sshhhh. Can you hear that sound? Listen very carefully. That's the sound of the ruling classes trembling at the threat of communistic revolution. So please allow me to introduce the terror of the bourgeois, the hobgoblin stalking Europe, the nightmare of greedy capitalists everywhere . . . without further ado . . . it's Dr Karl Marx!'

Everybody clapped enthusiastically and Dr Marx popped up from behind the podium, where he had been hiding all along. He was the hairiest man the pirates had ever seen.[14] Several of the crew were actually worried for a moment that the Seaweed That Walked Like a Man had returned from one of their previous adventures to ambush them. His nose was hairy. His forehead

---

14. While at university, Engels held a 'moustache evening' in which he invited all 'moustache-capable' young men to outrage philistines by growing moustaches and toasting their facial hair.

was hairy. Even his hands were hairy. And his beard was a great bushy black number, which looked like he had sellotaped a bunch of cats to the bottom of his face and then frightened them with a loud noise.

The Pirate Captain turned a shade of purple that, if you'd seen it on a flower petal rather than a pirate, would have been considered very becoming.

'I look nothing like him!' he exclaimed to the pirate in green, apoplectic. 'That beard! It looks like it's been scribbled on to his face by a toddler! And his ears! Do I have that much hair growing out of my ears?'

'No, Captain,' said the pirate in green. 'I've always admired how hairless your ears are.'

Marx cleared his throat, smiled and waited for the applause to die down.

'I love capitalism and think all the workers are lazy good-for-nothings who should be made to work until they die from exhaustion!'

The audience gasped.

'I don't really,' said Marx.

The communists sighed in relief. The pirates approved – the headline-grabbing opening line was a tried and tested pirate trick, much used by the Pirate Captain to get their attention. It suggested that they were in for a rollercoaster ride of a speech that would have them on the edge of their seats.

'I shall address you all tonight on the uprising of the Silesian weavers and how it can serve as an example for the urban proletariat in our struggle against the tyranny of the bourgeoisie.'

You can't exactly *hear* pirate expectations dropping, but if you could, everyone in Soho would have been deafened.

The Pirate Captain knew that it was bad form to doze off during a lecture. He wasn't sure how it had happened, but the next thing he knew he was waking up with his head on the pirate in green's shoulder. A thin stream of saliva had drooled out of his mouth.

'How long was I asleep?' he asked.

'About an hour,' said the pirate in green, fighting back a yawn. 'He's just getting warmed up, I think. It's quite ... erm, dry. You missed a heated discussion about whether communist paintings should restrict themselves to bleak geometric shapes' – he indicated a painting propped up on the podium that was mostly lines and triangles, but with the odd circle thrown in for light relief – 'or whether they should concentrate on stirring pictures of workers doing heroic things instead.' He indicated another painting that showed a rosy-cheeked peasant girl toiling in the wheat fields with the sun on her face who looked a bit tired, but in a sexy way that suggested she would still be a lot of fun to go out with. 'He tends to go off on tangents a lot. He's already spent

45

half an hour denouncing the man who decorated the room.'

'There will now be a short interval,' announced Marx. 'Comrade Engels will be serving ice cream by the doorway.'

Pirates and communists alike ran for the toilets. 'Ooh! Ice cream!' squealed Jennifer. There was a great crush of pirates towards the doorway, where Engels stood with a tray of ice cream round his neck.

'What flavours do you have?' asked the pirate with a hook for a hand.

'We have vanilla, strawberry and chocolate,' said Engels.

'Is that it? No raspberry ripple? That's my favourite.'

'Sorry.'

'When I saw *Cats!* they had cornettos. Why haven't you got cornettos?'

'I lost my little spoon out of the lid. Can I have another one?'

Eventually, the Pirate Captain got to the front of the queue. 'What flavours have you got then, comrade?' he asked with a grin.

'Pirate Captain! I'm so glad you came. We've got vanilla, strawberry and . . . *an important business proposition.*' Engels whispered this last part.

'What happened to the chocolate?' asked the Pirate Captain with a frown.

'Captain, this really is a matter of some urgency.'

'Yes, sorry. So. A business proposal. In pirate language that translates as "an idea for adventure", which I'm very keen on. Unless you meant a real business proposal, like a scam to buy and sell performing dogs to theatre impresarios – I don't like the idea of that one bit.'

'No, it's not that.'

'Good. Because it turns out that the market is sewn up,' said the Pirate Captain bitterly.

Engels ushered the Captain to one side. 'I take it that, being a pirate, you have a boat?'

'Best boat on the Seven Seas. Lord Nelson himself said it was the finest vessel he'd ever seen.'

Engels looked a little disbelieving. 'He didn't say it with his mouth,' the Captain added. 'He said it with his eyes. Eye.'

'I need to book passage to Paris for myself and Dr Marx. I fear we're in great peril.'

'Oh, I do peril very well,' said the Pirate Captain. 'It's practically my middle name. What kind of peril are you in? Haunted by ghosts? Caught impersonating a bishop? Chased by tigers?'

'Nothing like that,' said Engels, who was getting a bit impatient. His ice creams were melting and starting to make a little pink, yellow and brown pool on the floor.

'You're not being cooked in a pot by cannibals, are you?'

'No, Captain. There has been a series of terrible incidents of late. And it always seems to be us who get the blame. I believe that sinister forces are at work, and that Dr Marx's life may not be safe here in London. The atmosphere in this country . . . it's become something of a witch hunt.'

'Oh dear.'

'Oh dear indeed, Captain,' said Engels.

'But you're not witches? There's some way of telling which I can't really remember. I think it's if you can dive to the bottom of a swimming pool and successfully retrieve a brick whilst wearing a dressing gown, then you're a witch. But it might be the other way round.'

'We're not witches,' said Engels firmly. 'So, will you help?'

'To be honest, I've been thinking of an adventure more along the lines of pearl-smuggling in the South Seas or discovering a lost continent. We're being sponsored, you see, so it's got to be full of glamorous locations and scantily clad women. Carting a couple of communists over the Channel is a bit pedestrian for us.'

'Please, Captain! If we don't get to the safety of the Paris Commune, who knows what might happen! We can pay you well.'

'Oh, bad luck,' said the Pirate Captain sympathetically. 'If you'd said that in our last adventure, I'd have bitten your arm off.'

Engels didn't have a chance to try and persuade the Captain further, because the bell rang for the second half of the lecture and Dr Marx tramped back to his lectern with a heavy book.

The second half of the lecture wasn't much better than the first. The pirates were soon playing games of hangman and scratching their names into the benches. The pirate with a hook for a hand and the pirate with long legs entertained themselves by throwing little balls of rolled-up paper into a communist's collar, whilst the pirate with an earring passed notes to the pirate in green about the other pirates.

'...and that concludes why the latest Prussian censorship instruction is entirely symptomatic of the antiquated feudal-absolutist system. Now – any questions? I need to be certain that you've understood every single one of my arguments.'

Dr Marx looked slightly disappointed that the majority of the questions concerned themselves with less highbrow issues, such as whether it was true that Dr Marx habitually ate bourgeois babies in their cradles (it wasn't) and what hair products he used to create his magnificent mane of hair (Perkins' Radical's Pomade).

One or two pirates chipped in and asked how he proposed to deal with the dashing Pirate Captain and his nefarious band of buccaneers, but Dr Marx claimed to have never heard of them, before launching into a boring answer that drew an analogy between piracy and slum landlords. Eventually, an especially serious-looking statuesque blonde stood up at the front of the audience.

'I just wanted to congratulate Comrade Marx on his fine oratory,' said the statuesque blonde. 'And also to say that I've got your kittens.' She held up a soaking-wet sack.

'I beg your pardon?' said Marx, squinting down from his lectern.

'Your kittens.' The statuesque blonde paused and raised her voice. *'The ones that you asked me to drown in the canal.'*

The audience gasped.

'I really don't know what you're talking about,' protested Marx, looking flustered.

'But, Comrade Marx, you must remember! Of course you do. Why, it was only this morning you were saying to me how reactionary their TINY BUTTON NOSES and BRIGHT SHINY EYES were. And when you saw them innocently playing about with a ball of yarn, batting it back and forth between their ADORABLE LITTLE PAWS, you said that the only thing for it was to bundle them into a scratchy sack, ignoring their

HEART-RENDING MEWLING CRIES, and then go and drown them in the nearest canal.'

By this point, even the loyal communist audience was in an uproar, but the statuesque blonde went on shouting above the din. 'Anyhow, I just wanted you to know that I'd done it. And I stoved their heads in with a brick as well, just to make sure. You mentioned how you wanted the SAD, LIFELESS BODIES back for use as paperweights to keep your important philosophical notes together. So I'll just leave the sack here, shall I?'

This seemed to be the final straw for most of the audience, and they barged out of the room muttering that if Dr Marx proposed to bring about a world where decent folk feared for their kittens, then he could take his Communism and do something unmentionable with it.

'I've no idea who that statuesque young lady is!' Marx went on protesting from the podium. 'I've never seen her before in my life.'

A half-finished carton of ice cream sailed through the air, and he had to duck to avoid it. Soon it was followed by brass stuff from the ceiling, bits of seat and various pieces of taxidermy.

'Poor baby kittens!' said the albino pirate. I don't like these communists at all.'

'I'm more of a dog man, myself,' said the Pirate Captain. 'But even so. It's a bit much.'

Marx picked up the dripping sack and emptied it out onto the floor. Several of the pirates jumped back and covered their eyes, because they were worried that the skeleton kittens would give them nightmares, no matter what vestiges of adorableness remained. But all that spilled out was a pile of old fruit.

'You've turned the kittens into old fruit!' exclaimed the pirate in green. 'That's an amazing trick! Can you get the fruit to turn into doves?'

'No, you seem to be missing the point,' said Engels. 'That young lady was just trying to make Dr Marx look bad. Somebody stop her!'

Chasing sinister characters was all in a day's work for the pirates, and a group of them set off in hot pursuit of the mysterious blonde, but before long they traipsed back into the pub looking despondent.

'We did our best,' said the pirate with a hook for a hand, a little out of breath. 'Only she leapt into a waiting hansom cab, which clattered off atmospherically into the fog. But we caught a glimpse of the driver. He was a giant! Swathed in a billowing cape, and with demonic glowing eyes!'

'He was bigger than Scurvy Jake!' exclaimed the albino pirate. Scurvy Jake was the biggest pirate any of the pirates had ever met. 'Or even two Scurvy Jakes, with one Scurvy Jake standing on top of the other Scurvy Jake's shoulders!'

'If he was a font,' said the pirate in green, 'he would be about a hundred point! If font size goes up that far.

And if he was a type of cheese, he'd be one of those big wheels of Cheddar that they roll down hills.'

The Captain grimaced, and gave Marx an apologetic shrug. 'I'm sorry about this. The lads have an unfortunate tendency to exaggerate. I think it's because there's too much sugar in their diet.' He turned back to his crew. 'I've warned you about this before; exaggerating things might seem like fun, but it can be very dangerous. Remember the time I asked if we had enough milk onboard, and you all said, "Oh, yes, there's loads of milk left, Captain," but there wasn't, and I had to spend half the voyage eating my Weetabix with butter?'

'Honestly, Captain, we're not exaggerating this time,' said the albino pirate, his lip trembling.

'It hardly matters now,' said Marx, dusting himself down. 'It's clear that we cannot stay in London a moment longer. What with this and the claims that I put up the entry price at the zoo, I fear we need to get out tonight.' He pulled a stuffed sparrow out of his mane.

'So, Pirate Captain, you see our predicament. Will you help?' asked Engels.

The Pirate Captain thought for a moment. Engels and Marx looked at him pleadingly. He sighed, and despite himself felt his craggy heart melt a bit. 'Aaarrrr,' he said. 'Maybe it's not quite as exotic an adventure as I was hoping for. But I can't say I approve of these sinister characters' methods. And besides, what are us pirates famous for?'

'Scurvy?' suggested Engels.

'Roaring?' suggested Marx.

'Being good at tying knots?' suggested the pirate in green.

'No, we're famous for our pronounced sense of fair play,' said the Captain cheerily. 'But don't worry. That was what they call a rhetorical question, so I'm not surprised you didn't get it.'

Five

THE CRUSTACEAN
CARNIVAL OF FEAR

'It's taken me years to realise it, Pirate Captain, but you are actually the best at pirating.' Black Bellamy looked at his drink and frowned.

'And?' said the Pirate Captain.

'And the best dancer, the most debonair and the best at knowing about cuisine. I'm just a big loser with a beard that goes all the way up to my eyes.'

'Don't be so hard on yourself,' said the Pirate Captain. 'You've done well, in your own small way. But being my nemesis was never going to work out, was it? For all your cunning and mischief, you've simply come up against a better man. With a better hat. In Hawaii.'

The Pirate Captain stretched out on his sun lounger and sipped grog from a coconut. Black Bellamy slunk off.

'Crestfallen,' said the Pirate Captain, savouring the word. With a click of his elegant fingers, a lanky woman in a bikini strolled over and started massaging the Pirate Captain's shoulders. He passed a languid gaze over the swimming pool, where some of the pirates were splashing about and having fun.

Oh look, some dancing hams, he thought. A line of hams and steaks shimmied past the Pirate Captain, dancing little waltzes and tangos. He grabbed one as it went past and sunk his teeth into its glistening flesh. But instead of the warm meaty flavour of well-roasted ham, he got a mouthful of feathers.

'Mmpphhh,' said the Pirate Captain, waking with a start. The pirate with a scarf stood at his bedside with a glass of water.

'Dancing hams again, sir?'

'Mff-mffruff-ffooh,' said the Pirate Captain.

'You might want to take the pillow out of your mouth.'[15]

Tramping out of his cabin and opening the bathroom door to billowing clouds of steam, the Pirate Captain

---

15. The animal with the longest period of REM sleep, the state commonly associated with dreams, is the armadillo. Nobody knows what armadillos dream about, probably ants, of which they can eat up to 40,000 for a single meal.

was pleased to see that his trusty number two had already run him a bath. He stripped off his pyjamas and was just about to put a toe in the water, when he saw that a terrible hairy sea creature was already sat in it. The Pirate Captain leapt backwards in horror, grabbing for something to hit the sea creature with. He found himself waving a bar of soap as menacingly as possible.

'Do you have any more shower gel?' asked the sea creature, waggling an empty bottle of shower gel at the Captain. 'I seem to have used this all up.'

The Pirate Captain goggled, and then decided that he really wasn't in any state for this sort of thing. He backed out of the door and bumped into the pirate with a scarf carrying some towels.

'I don't know if this is one of those times when my dream hasn't ended even though I supposed it had,' said the Captain to the pirate with a scarf. 'But there appears to be some kind of sea creature in there. Probably crawled in through a porthole. And now it's washing itself in my bath.'

'Yes, sir. I meant to warn you. Except it's not a sea creature. It's Dr Marx.'

'Are you sure? It really is very, very hairy.'

'Yes, Captain. It seems to grow out of all of him. I've not seen anything like it before.'

'He's used up all my shower gel,' said the Captain indignantly. 'The good stuff that keeps my skin soft and comes in a bottle shaped like a dolphin.'

'I tried to explain that it was your private bathroom, Captain. But he didn't seem to be listening.'

'Excuse me,' bellowed Marx.

The Pirate Captain opened the bathroom door again. 'Hello, yes?'

'What sort of time do you do breakfast around here?'

The Captain shrugged. 'Oh well, you know, whenever. We're fairly relaxed about that sort of thing.'

'I'll be wanting orange juice, but not with bits in.' Marx rubbed himself vigorously with the Captain's best loofah. 'I don't like bits.'

'Right, I'll, uh, see what we've got to hand,' said the Captain, feeling slightly at a loss. 'Um. So. You're all right for towels?'

'Yes, thanks,' said the hairy communist.

The Pirate Captain backed out of the bathroom, whilst Marx struck up a rousing chorus of the Internationale.

The Captain paced up and down the deck, looking dour and drinking his morning tea. The pirate with a scarf hurried along beside him, struggling to keep up with his gigantic strides. Normally, they took this time to tackle the tricky business of running the boat, but the Pirate Captain's mind was elsewhere.

'I counted the portholes like you asked me to,

Captain,' said the pirate with a scarf. 'There are still thirty-six of them; no change from last week.'

'Do you know what my bath was like this morning after he'd left?' said the Captain, with a scowl. 'Full of thick black hairs. Enough to knit a cardigan. A scratchy Marx-hair cardigan.'

'I don't much fancy that, sir,' said the pirate with a scarf.

'And you'll notice I'm not drinking from my favourite mug,' the Pirate Captain went on, indicating his mug. The Pirate Captain's favourite mug was one he'd got from a garden centre. It had a picture of a flea on the side that only appeared when it had a hot drink in it. This one just had 'Monkey World' emblazoned across the handle and was about his fifth favourite. 'Because *somebody* was using it. Then, when he was lounging about on a deckchair a bit later, he asked if I could sail the boat at a slightly different angle, because he was getting the sun in his eyes.'

'I much preferred that nice Mr Darwin,' said the pirate with a scarf.

'Me too. At least he didn't look like a cat crossed with a monkey.' The Captain let out an indignant snort. 'But he's a paying guest. And I suppose it's not really the done thing to run through paying guests.'

'No, Captain.'

'And stuffing him into a cannon and firing him into the sun would probably be out of the question as well?'

'I don't think the Pirate King would approve,' said the pirate with a scarf ruefully. 'You know how seriously he takes the issue of good manners.'

'Damn our piratical code of hospitality.'

'It can be a burden, sir.'

'Worse still, there's no wind! And that's important, isn't it? Because . . .' The Pirate Captain scratched his cheek as he tried to remember something.

'Because it makes the boat go along, sir?' said the pirate with a scarf.

'That's the one. A little test for you there, number two.' He patted the pirate with a scarf on the head. 'So no wind means we won't go along for some time. Which means I have to put up with that ungrateful lubber for even longer. I'm really starting to feel the strain. Look at my eyes.' The Pirate Captain opened his eyes wide and offered them to the pirate with a scarf.

'They're very slightly bloodshot, sir.'

'Exactly. I'm a wreck. I wouldn't be surprised if I died from the mental pressure.'[16] He sighed. And then, seeing Marx bounding across the deck towards them, did his best to try and return his face to its customary pleasant openness. Engels followed alongside, sniffing into a handkerchief.

---

16. Philosopher John Stuart Mill had a nervous breakdown (caused by too much thinking at an early age), but he was cured by hanging around with Harriet Taylor, a girl whom he fancied and later married. Despite this, he still thought intellectual and cultural pleasures were superior to physical ones.

'I'm sorry to say it, Captain,' said Marx. 'But our situation is unacceptable. Do you think we are animals?'

Yes, I do, thought the Pirate Captain. Very much. You've hit the nail on the head there. And not even a good type of animal. But he managed to force a winning smile. 'Something wrong?' he enquired politely.

'Engels and I,' said Marx. 'We simply cannot be expected to share quarters. I'm a thinker, Pirate Captain. And for thinking I need plenty of personal space. Do you realise that I had to make Engels sleep up here on the deck last night? On the deck! Of a ship! I couldn't even give him a pillow, because I need a minimum of three pillows.'

'Oh well, sleeping on the deck, that can be quite fun,' said the pirate with a scarf. 'You get to watch the stars, and listen to the ocean. It's like camping. Sometimes we sit out and cook marshmallows on a little fire. Though we've stopped that now, because it turns out "lighting fires" and "wooden boats" aren't an ideal mix.'

'Honestly, it's really not a problem,' said Engels, looking embarrassed by the whole thing.

'Nonsense!' said Marx. 'He's caught a cold. And he's not much use to me sneezing all over my papers.'

'Dear me. Well, I suppose we do have a room he can use,' said the Pirate Captain. He shot the pirate with a scarf a pained look and led them below deck.

Beneath the creaking boards, the Pirate Captain unlocked a door and threw it back to reveal a tiny cabin.

There was a bed with a duvet covered in sporting scenes, posters on the walls of animals and baseball players, and a great pile of children's toys, none of which had been taken out of their wrapping.

'Here you go,' said the Pirate Captain.

'Ah . . . this seems to be occupied,' said Engels, backing away.

'Sadly, no,' sighed the Pirate Captain. 'This cabin is for the son I never had. See? There's his baseball bat. He'd have been quite the athlete, but he'd love animals too, and just look at the books he'd read. I'd have called him Champ. "Come here, Champ," I'd say and we'd probably do a bit of rough-housing.' He demonstrated some rough-housing on the pirate with a scarf.

'Anyhow,' the Captain added, 'I hope you'll both be joining us for dinner?'

Marx prodded unenthusiastically at his boiled cabbage.

'I'd heard,' he said, sounding a little put out, 'that you pirate types tended to enjoy gargantuan and debauched feasts. I suppose I've been misinformed.'

'No, you're quite right,' said the Pirate Captain, looking pretty unenthused by his bit of cabbage as well. 'Sometimes they go on for days, and we actually end up having smaller feasts in between the courses of the main feast. It can get quite complicated. Normally they're such a high point of an adventure that whoever we're helping out gets a laminated certificate saying "I had a feast with the pirates on one of their adventures". We just thought, what with you going on about how you didn't have any truck with all that material-wealth business, and how much you admired the common street-sweeper sort, that you'd prefer something like this.'

Marx shook his bushy head and pushed his plate away. 'On the contrary. That is my curse, Pirate Captain. Oh! What I wouldn't give to be a noble member of the proletariat! How I'd love to enjoy their simple pleasures and plain, uninspired meals. But I am for ever tainted by my breeding, doomed by my sensitive palate to enjoy only the best food and the finest cigars.'

'Oh well, that's a bit of a relief,' said the Captain, brightening up. 'See, I was actually eating this steak off my lap. And I had this gravy hidden in my sleeve.' He shook his sleeve and a few dollops of gravy fell out. The rest of the pirates took out the plates of food that they had been hiding under the table.

The pirate in green coughed. 'So,' he said to Marx, 'how did you get into philosophising? Did you run away and join a band of travelling thinkers? Or were you raised in the woods by wild philosophers?'

'No, sir. I started out as a journalist,' said Marx, happily helping himself to some grilled puffin and humming-bird skewers.

'Really? Well, that's a coincidence,' said the Pirate

Captain. 'I'm a journalist of sorts myself. I write a newsletter for my fans. They're lubbers, but they call themselves the Cutlass Club – they get a three-colour badge on joining. Do you give your communists badges?'

'It's not just a *club*, Pirate Captain,' said Marx stiffly. 'It's an international uprising of the proletariat.'

'People love badges,' said the Pirate Captain.

At the other end of the table, Engels turned to the pirate with a scarf. 'What's it like being a working pirate?' he asked quietly. 'I must say that your captain isn't quite what I was expecting.'

'Oh, well. He's a very busy man,' said the pirate with a scarf. 'He doesn't really have time to worry about the details.'

'I see. And how does that affect the rest of you?'

'It . . . can be . . . a little demanding on my time,' said the pirate with a scarf. 'But I wouldn't want it any other way. The Captain is a brilliant man. Though he can be a bit crabby in the mornings.'[17]

'Why does he keep laughing whenever I say any-thing?'

'He seems to think that you're the funny one out of

---

17. Don't listen to people telling you that getting up early is best. René Descartes is one of history's most important philosophers, but he rarely got out of bed before noon – and when he started getting up early for a new job as a private tutor, it caused him to catch pneumonia and die.

you and Marx. He's convinced you're some sort of double act and that you're only there for comic relief.'

Engels looked sadly at his chicken-stuffed-with-a-smaller-chicken. 'He's not the first, but . . . Well, Dr Marx is a brilliant man too. I . . . ' He went a bit quiet.

'Of course, in addition to being a pirate and a bit of a journalist, I'm also something of a philosopher,' said the Pirate Captain.

'Really?' said Marx.

'In fact,' said the Pirate Captain, warming to his theme, 'I'd go so far as to say that my adventures are as much an intellectual journey as an actual journey. Take the one where we went to Poland – we had to disguise ourselves as chess pieces. They're quite intellectual, aren't they?'

'I don't mean to be rude,' said Marx, because that's what people say when they mean to be rude, 'but do you really think a *pirate* can have much to add to the canon of Western thought?'

'It might surprise you to learn that I have a deep and considered philosophy,' said the Pirate Captain, in his best measured tones. 'It's mainly a meat-based theory. I feel that everybody should strive to eat as much red meat as possible. That's one tenet. Another would be that I tend to know best. And my third tenet – I always think it's best to have three – is probably something to do with the ocean. Generally I would say that I'm in favour of it.'

As a gesture of goodwill, upon coming aboard the boat Engels had given the whole crew a copy of Marx's latest book. A few of them had flicked through it that morning, though it was soon glaringly obvious that it didn't contain any swordfights or racy descriptions of fiery Latin princesses. But it was quite a thick book, and the pirates approved of the thwacking sound it made when you crept up on another pirate and smacked him round the head with it.

The Pirate Captain now put down his fork and opened Marx's book at a random page. 'You see, you've done well to write all this,[18] and some of it's pretty good. This "each according to his abilities to each according to his needs" thing makes a lot of sense. For instance, I often *need* a clean plate, but my *ability* to do the washing-up is rather limited. I'm just not very thorough. So it makes a lot more sense to get one of the lads to do it. But I can't say I agree with all your arguments. Here's your first problem,' he said, pointing at a sentence. '"Religion is the opium of the people." Well, I don't know about people, but I think you'll find the opium of pirates is actual opium.'

---

18. Probably the most prolific philosopher was St Thomas Aquinas, who wrote approximately 8 million words, which is equivalent to about 260 pirate books.

'I'm not sure you've really grasped my philosophical points,' said Marx.

'And this next part is patently absurd. "You have nothing to lose except your chains." It's true, I am always losing my chains, but that's just the start of it. I also lose the anchors that tend to be attached to my chains. I can never find my reading glasses. And I doubt a day goes by when I don't forget where I've put my astrolabe.'

'When Black Bellamy tricked you into wearing that gigantic nappy,' added the albino pirate, 'you lost your dignity then.'

'Exactly,' said the Captain. 'The list of things we have to lose is virtually endless.'

Marx grimaced. 'I'm afraid philosophy is not something lesser minds would really understand.'

'All that "if I drop a cannonball and a bag of feathers off a tree in the middle of a forest but nobody is about to see it then who's to say if I'm actually eating this ham?" business – how hard can it be?'

'I think,' said Marx, 'you probably underestimate the effort involved in the writing of a major philosophical work.'

'Aarrrr,' said the Pirate Captain, raising one eyebrow and tapping his gold tooth with his thumb. Unbeknownst to Marx and Engels, this seemingly innocuous gesture was actually a sign that the Pirate Captain had *come up with something*. The pirate crew's faces were variously:

1. Thrilled. The pirates who liked surprises couldn't wait to hear what it was. Many of them still remembered the time the Pirate Captain had decided they should turn the pirate boat into a giant sledge and 'go down mountains and stuff'.
2. Wary. The more experienced pirates knew that this could signal absolutely anything. Like the time they had used the converted pirate boat to sledge down Mont Blanc and ended up in a lake full of man-eating alligators.
3. Covered in meat juice.

'What are pirates famous for?' asked the Pirate Captain, with a grin.

Marx chewed on his food for a moment. 'Plunder? Shanties? Your pronounced sense of fair play?' he suggested.

'No – we're mainly famous for our *wagers*,' said the Pirate Captain. 'So then, a friendly challenge – by the end of this voyage I will have written a work of philosophy that changes Western thought once and for all! You do the same, and the one that's most world-changing wins.'

Marx banged his puffin leg on the table. 'You, sir, have yourself a wager!' he cried. 'If you win, I shall have Engels here shine your shoes.'

'Best get philosophising then. But not before pudding, obviously. Did you say you liked cigars?' The Pirate Captain handed him a box of cigars. Marx sniffed at one.

'Rolled on the dusky inner thighs of a native Cuban girl?'

'I don't think so. But we could roll them on the pirate with a scarf's inner thighs if you wanted,' suggested the Pirate Captain. 'He keeps them quite smooth. He won't mind at all.'

Six

I WAS A SLAVE OF
THE SEA LIONS

By the next morning the Pirate Captain had hit a bit of a wall. He'd spend half the night on his major work, but it wasn't really coming together.[19] It didn't help that every time he got to a tricky bit, he'd play a couple of hands of solitaire or waste half an hour trying on hats. He'd had the boat sailing in circles for a while now, to give himself more time to finish, and he really didn't know how much longer he could keep it up before Marx suspected something.

There was a knock at the door, and then the pirate

---

19. A tip for students of philosophy: writing philosophy is quite tricky. You need to make a cogent and logical argument based on accepted premises. You can't just get away with reading a bit of someone else's work and then vehemently disagreeing with it to hide the fact you don't really know what you're talking about.

with a monobrow came in, followed by a small group of other pirates. They looked a bit shifty.

'Hello, lads,' said the Captain, grateful for the distraction. 'Something I can help you with?'

'Yes, Captain,' said the pirate with the monobrow, trying his best to look resolute. 'A few of us pirates have been listening to Dr Marx, and we have come to the conclusion that we, the workers, are being unfairly oppressed.'

There was a pause. If the pirates had been around 150 years later they would probably have recognised it as a 'Pinteresque' pause, as menacing as any zombie. Not quite as menacing maybe, because *The Pirates! In an Adventure with a Menacing Pause* wouldn't be much cop. But, still, menacing nonetheless.

'Is that so?' said the Pirate Captain eventually, almost imperceptibly arching an eyebrow. 'Is that what they're calling pirates who spend all afternoon lazing about the deck trying to see how many starfish they can balance on top of each other, these days? "Workers"?'

'We don't think it's right that we should have to tie knots in bits of rope and swab the decks, whilst you lie idle, growing fat on the profits of our labours.'

'I don't think I'll grow fat on bits of rope, do you? No matter how nicely you've tied knots in them.'

'Tell him the list of demands,' whispered the pirate in red before ducking out of view.

'Demands, eh? That sounds serious. Well, I suppose we'd better hear them.'

The pirate with a monobrow began to recite his list. 'One: an end to the use of derogatory phrases such as "you scurvy landlubbers" when ordering us about. Because when you think about it, it doesn't even make much sense, seeing as how landlubbers don't tend to get scurvy. Two: more of a say on what we eat at feasts. Perhaps we could be a little more adventurous with our choice of meats? Three: when you read us a bedtime story, we were hoping it could be something other than your unpublished novel? Oh, yes, and four: a more equal distribution of cereal from mini variety packs.'

The Pirate Captain steepled his fingers in front of his face. 'I think your manifesto contains some very salient points,' he said after another long pause. 'And to show that I'm not an unreasonable man, I'm going to let you all off doing the washing-up today, and instead we're going to play a new game I've just invented a moment ago.'

Some of the stupider pirates who weren't too good at reading between the lines or picking up on disagreeable undertones cheered at this news. The pirate with a monobrow looked a bit uncomfortable.

'I think I'm going to call it Pop-up Pirate,' said the Captain, leading them out on to the deck. 'How it works is like this: you go and hide in that barrel. The rest of us take turns to poke our cutlasses through the sides of the aforementioned barrel, and the first one to make you jump up in the air gets a prize.'

A few minutes later, the game was over. The pirate with a monobrow hadn't jumped up at all.

'Oh dear. Look at that,' said the Captain, peering over the top of the barrel. 'He's all stabbed. Well, there's always going to be a few teething troubles with these new games. Do you think Scrabble got where it is today without a few fatalities along the way? Anyhow, back to those demands. Does anybody else think they could do a better job of running the boat than me?'

The revolutionary pirates looked at their shoes.

'Mm. I thought as much. If I hear another paean to the gnarly-handed worker I might not be responsible for my actions. Now, go and do that washing-up.'

The pirates started to leave.

'Not you,' said the Pirate Captain, glowering at the pirate in red. 'I've got a job for you.'

The pirate in red managed to look guilty and surly at the same time.

'I don't want to play another round of Pop-up Pirate right now, but I'm pretty fickle and you never know when the mood will take me. So I want you to take these ship's biscuits to Dr Marx and see if you can find out how he's getting on with his major work of philosophy. Then back here, pronto.'

The pirate in red stood outside Marx's cabin with a plate of pink wafers. He knocked on the door.

'What is it?' barked Marx. Inside, the cabin was a complete tip, with books strewn across the floor, cigar ash spilling out of ashtrays and half-drunk mugs of tea everywhere. The remains of Marx's lunch were pushed under the hammock. In the centre of it all paced the philosopher, his brow furrowed and his hair sticking up from where he'd been yanking it in frustration.

'I've brought you some ship's biscuits, courtesy of the Captain.'

'Oh, yes. Well, leave them there on the table,' said Marx, going back to his brow-furrowing.

The pirate in red sidled over to the desk. 'I'd just like to say that I'm a great admirer of your work, Dr Marx.'

'Is that so?' said Marx, breaking into a broad smile.

'Yes, I like the bits with equations best.'

'I'm very proud of them.'

'How is the major work going?'

'To be honest, I've barely started.' Marx slumped into a chair. 'I seem to keep distracting myself with games of solitaire and by trying on different hats.' A pile of hats lay in the corner.

'Do you think you'll be done by the time we get to France?'

'I'm afraid not,' said Marx glumly. He picked up a wafer. 'These biscuits, they're not doctored, are they? You know, like with racehorses. The Pirate Captain wouldn't try to nobble me with knock-out drops or something?'

'Oh, no, nothing like that. The Pirate Captain is more of a . . . straightforward intellect. He's asked us to sail around in circles for a bit so that he has more time to finish.'

'Ah, thank you for that.'

'Well, I'll be off then. Cheerio,' said the pirate in red.

'Yes. Cheerio,' said Marx.

'So he's nearly finished,' said the pirate in red.

The Pirate Captain fiddled anxiously with one of his epaulettes. 'Really?'

'Oh, yes – he was just finishing Appendix Four when I walked in. It looked pretty impressive – a nice thick manuscript and everything.'

'Hell's barnacles!' said the Pirate Captain. 'Looks like an all-nighter for me then. I think five days to sail twenty miles is pushing it a bit.' He stirred a few more spoonfuls of instant coffee into his mug.

Bleary-eyed, the Pirate Captain bundled together his manuscript and ran up on to the deck. He was met by the whole crew waiting for the unveiling of the two major works of philosophy. There was something of the spirit of carnival amongst the pirates, and several had made banners and bunting. It wasn't every day that the pirate boat saw a pageant of intellectual endeavour. Some of the pirates were so excited that they'd been sent back to bed to calm themselves down.

None of it really helped the Pirate Captain's mood. Yesterday's attempted revolution hadn't worked, but he didn't want to look bad in front of the men when such feelings were aboard. Despite spending the whole night finishing his major work, he wasn't sure that it would pass Marx's rigorous intellectual standards. The grumpy philosopher was already on deck, in a huddle with a flustered-looking Engels.

'Before we do this, I'd like to point out that I'd written much more,' the Captain started to explain, 'but it vanished in the night. Probably eaten by weevils. Terrible problem on a boat, weevils are.'[20]

Marx didn't seem to be listening. He held up his hand. 'Pirate Captain, I'm afraid I am going to have to admit defeat. I've not managed much more than this . . .'

He opened his book and showed a single page. It was completely blank, apart from a short paragraph in German and a few geometric doodles in the margin. Marx's hairy face almost looked humble.

---

20. Ship's biscuits would be baked three times, in order to make it as tough as possible for weevils to burrow into them. An unfortunate side effect of this is that when you're seven years old and you go on a school visit to HMS Victory and they give you an authentic ship's biscuit and you try to take a great big bite out of it, chances are you'll lose a tooth and end up crying for the rest of the trip.

'Oh,' said the Pirate Captain. 'I'm sure it's very good. What does it mean?'

'It means nothing, sir. It's little more than the lyrics to a song that I couldn't get out of my head all night.'

'Ah. Well, I've finished mine. But don't feel bad – it's probably not all that.'

The Pirate Captain handed over his hastily stapled-together wodge of papers. The front cover featured a picture of the Pirate Captain leaning on a gate and looking clever, beneath the title *The Wit and Wisdom of the Pirate Captain*. A ragged cheer erupted from the assembled pirates, and they waved their flags.

'All right, lads, give it a rest,' said the Pirate Captain. He'd rather they didn't make things worse by raising everybody's expectations.

Marx cracked open the book and started reading. 'You can't have a rainbow . . . without a little rain,' read Marx slowly. He turned the page and read on. 'By observing the natural world, we can deduce that the best way to impress girls is by being aloof, then funny, then deep – in that order.' Marx licked a finger and turned the page again. 'It is my opinion that there are several different kinds of face. There are "plate" faces, which are flat with upturned chins. There are "potatoes", which are shapeless and may be lumpy. There are "lion" type faces, which tend to have flat, broad noses and—' Marx stopped, and fixed the Pirate Captain with a serious stare. 'Is this all your work, Pirate Captain?'

The Pirate Captain looked sheepish. 'Yes. It's just a first draft, you realise.'

'But it's brilliant!' exclaimed Marx, slapping his forehead. 'It's . . .' He leafed furiously through the book. 'There's all sorts here – recipes, jokes, puzzles, little observations . . . and what's this? A list of what's hot and what's not!'

'I do a new one every so often,' said the Pirate Captain.

'So do I! I tend to stick to philosophers and macroeconomic trends, but it's the same principle! Oh, Pirate Captain, we have more in common than I realised!'

'You really like it?'

'It's a triumph! I love the "pick it up and put it down" approach. I could keep this in my toilet and edify visitors to my house. This is astounding!'

'I think I've misjudged you,' said the Pirate Captain.

'And I you,' said Marx. 'You see, Engels? This is where I've been going wrong – why, *Das Kapital* didn't even have a *single* page to colour in!'

'Oh, look,' said the Pirate Captain, 'there's Paris.' He beamed.

Seven

WHY WON'T THESE MER-PEOPLE JUST LEAVE ME ALONE?

Paris in those days also had its fair share of cholera-ridden hags and infant death and mud, but the cholera-ridden hags coughed with slightly more continental élan, and the infant death only seemed to strike the uglier babies. The mud was pretty much the same. Even though the pirates didn't have any real reason to be disguised, several of them had cut their hair into chic bobs and bought themselves tiny dogs to carry about. The pirate in red pointed out how useful the Pirate Captain's French language skills would prove to be now they were actually in France, but the Pirate Captain said that he spoke such a complex dialect the Parisians probably wouldn't be able to understand him, so in fact he would be sticking to English for the duration of their visit, and anybody who was minded to bring the subject up again would be advised to keep quiet.

'I suppose,' said the Pirate Captain to Marx, as they strolled down a leafy boulevard, with Engels and the pirate with a scarf hefting their luggage a little way behind, 'that there's some clever way we get in touch with these Paris communists? Something to do with code words inserted into the *Le Monde* crossword? "Three across – the swallow flies east tonight". "Shadowy meetings in the park". That kind of thing?'

'No, Pirate Captain,' replied Marx. 'We're on the more enlightened continent now, where we communists are not vilified like in London. In fact, a group of my followers have set up the Paris Commune, as a sort of utopian model of how society should be, lived according to my philosophical principles.'[21]

'A utopian society!' said the albino pirate excitedly.

'With lady models! And as much meat as you can eat!'

'And furniture made from that Spanish ham that tastes of fruit!'

'And intelligent, talking dogs that brush your teeth for you!'

The pirates all got so carried away with imagining what a perfect utopian society would be like that they

---

21. The Soviet spaceflight Voskhod 1 took a fragment of a banner from the Paris Commune into space. A fragment of the Jolly Roger has yet to go into space, presumably because the pirate space programme is not very advanced.

didn't even notice that they'd already arrived at the Commune. It was a bit of a let-down. But the pirates tried their best to hide their disappointment.[22]

'Funny sort of utopia,' muttered the Pirate Captain, pulling away some of the peeling paint from the door. A hand-written sign said 'No door-to-door salesmen, no circulars and no bourgeois oppression'. Marx rang the bell, and before long a baleful-looking eye appeared at the peephole and peered out at them. Then there was the sound of several bolts being drawn back, and the door creaked open to reveal a French communist in a beret.

'Comrades!' boomed Marx, ushering the pirates into the hallway. 'These are my new friends. This is the Pirate Captain, and these are his aquatic crew. I know they look like questionable types, but the Pirate Captain here is a fellow philosopher.'

'Hello, pirates,' said the communists.

'Hello, communists,' said the pirates.

After that, the conversation lapsed a bit. Normally, the Pirate Captain would put this down to how bad his crew were at mingling with non-work people, but in this instance he had to partly blame the communists. They seemed glum, especially for a group of people living in

---

22. Thomas More coined the term 'Utopia' in his book Libellus vere aureus, nec minus salutaris quam festivas, de optimo reipublicae statu deque nova insula Utopia of 1516. Though of course his version is flawed, because it was written over four hundred years before the young Julie Christie and tubs of Häagen-Dazs even existed.

a utopia. Nobody was singing, or laughing, or even reading out stirring political poetry. Mostly the French communists looked like somebody had just that second told them the truth about Santa.

'Things haven't been going well in London,' said Marx. 'We've had to flee because someone is trying to ruin our reputation.'

'Oh, dear me. It's the same here,' said one of the communists miserably. 'All sorts of terrible things have been happening, and we seem to get the blame for everything.'

By way of explanation the communist indicated a stack of old newspapers piled up on the coffee table. Marx's eyes flicked across the headlines.

THE HIGH PRICE OF TINY DOGS LATELY – COMMUNISTS TO BLAME?

ARE OUR BOULEVARDS NOT SO WIDE AND LEAFY AS THEY WERE? COMMUNISTS!

IS THE RED MENACE BEHIND THIS WEATHER WE'VE BEEN HAVING?

'It goes on in the same vein. Just last week we were accused of stealing nine bears from the Paris zoo. What would we do with nine bears?' said the communist, sounding a little exasperated.

'You could get them to form one of those human

pyramid things, except with bears, instead of humans,' suggested the Pirate Captain. 'Actually, you'd only need six bears to make a pyramid, but the other three could be spares.'

'We didn't steal any bears.'

'That's a pity. I'd have liked to have seen a bear pyramid.'

'This is bleak,' said Marx, shaking his bushy beard. 'My reputation back in England is in tatters, and now I find out that our troubles seem to have followed us here to France.'

'Would you like to hear my considered philosophical opinion, Marx?' said the Pirate Captain, trying to lighten the mood.

'By all means, Captain.'

'I think of it like this – there are only two certainties in life. One is the inevitability of death, and the other is *uncertainty itself*. So when everything seems to be going badly, it's probably meant to be. Or perhaps it's fate. Either way, it's something we'll never really know, and it doesn't pay to waste too much time thinking about it. Eat a chop instead.'

'Dr Marx,' said Jennifer. 'it's obvious you and your communists have a lot to discuss, and we were thinking that it might be nice for us pirates to see a few sights.'

'Yes, good idea,' said the Pirate Captain. 'A lot of people follow our adventures with a view to getting travel tips and ideas, because we go to so many exotic climes.

So I think it's only right that whilst we're here in Paris we check out the local attractions.'

'While your pirates do that, perhaps you would accompany me to the salon?' said Marx to the Pirate Captain.

The Pirate Captain looked a bit dubious at this suggestion. 'Is that a salon like we have in England, where you go to get a fancy new haircut? It's just that I never let anybody but the pirate with a scarf cut my hair. Between you, me and the gatepost, I have a slightly funny-shaped head, and if I'm not careful I end up looking like that Nefertiti bust. He does these clever feathery bits, hides it very well.'

'Yes, I see. But you needn't worry. It's not like one of those salons, but rather a place where the Parisian élite go to discuss intellectual matters of the day. It will be a fantastic introduction of your philosophies to the wider world.' Marx clapped the Captain on the back. 'And I must confess to a selfish interest, because I have a feeling that by bringing you along, I may be able to restore my popularity.'

'Oh, well, that's different. It sounds right up my street,' said the Pirate Captain. 'I love intellectual matters of the day.'

The pirate with a scarf held up his hand, looking a little anxious. 'Pirate Captain, do you think sitting about in a Paris salon talking about stuff counts as an adventure any more than sitting about in London did?'

The Captain clicked his tongue thoughtfully. 'Hmmm . . . I suppose not. What does the small print on the Perkins contract say?'

The pirate with a scarf pulled the contract from his pocket. 'It says that the . . . ah . . . blah, blah . . . "aforementioned adventure of which the full part is to be sponsored by the party of the first part must involve running through, deathly peril, a racy encounter, at least one chase, numerous incidents of bloodthirstiness, a few shanties and a comic bit with some creatures".'

'Nothing about pontificating on the meaning of life?'

'No, sir.'

'And I don't suppose that a *metaphorical* running through of a poorly constructed argument is going to do the trick, is it?'

'It explicitly says in Clause 45b that metaphorical running through will not suffice.'

'Well, not to worry,' said the Captain, with a grin. 'You know what we're like. We're bound to run into trouble.'

The pirates couldn't agree which was the best thing to see in Paris, so they split into groups. One group decided to go to Madame Tussauds to see the waxworks. Another group decided to go to the Louvre to see the paintings. And the third group decided to go to the Folies Bergère to see the ladies who left nothing to the imagination. The Pirate Captain took the precaution of making sure each group took a packed lunch with them and learnt from the communists how to ask a policeman for help in case they got into any trouble.

The pirates who went to the Louvre were a bit disappointed to find that the gallery didn't seem to have a single one of those pictures of the girl with green skin, or of unicorns standing on a giant chessboard in space.

'Why do you suppose they painted so many bowls of fruit in the olden days?' said the pirate who liked kittens and sunsets, stifling a yawn. 'Why not bowls of ham?'

'Yes. It doesn't exactly encourage healthy eating habits,' agreed the pirate with gout.

'These Pre-Raphaelite girls certainly look like they could do with a bit more red meat in their diet. Look how pasty they are,' said the pirate with a nut allergy.

'Oooh! This next room contains the *Mona Lisa*,' said the pirate with a scarf, looking at his guide. 'Who, according to this, is "one of the most enigmatic ladies ever painted".'[23]

'Does enigmatic mean not wearing a thing?'

---

23. A recent analysis of the Mona Lisa using emotional-recognition software showed her to be eighty-three per cent happy, six per cent fearful, two per cent angry and nine per cent disgusted.

'No. You know when the Pirate Captain says something like, "I may lead a secret double life as a spy? Or maybe I don't. Who's to say?" and then he arches an eyebrow? That's enigmatic.'

'Ah. I always thought that was just annoying.'

There was quite a crowd in front of the *Mona Lisa*, and it took the pirates a little while to fight their way through. They all looked up excitedly, and this is what they saw:

Communists are the best

'Well, I suppose it's OK. Though I'm not sure I can *really* see what all the fuss is about,' said the pirate with long legs.

'It lacks a certain something,' said the pirate with gout.

'This Leonardo da Vinci,' said the pirate with a scarf. 'He was supposed to be a genius, was he?'

'Someone's stolen the *Mona Lisa*!' shouted an adorable French child.

'Another outrage by those filthy communists,' said a gigantic statuesque blonde. 'They won't stop until they have brought civilisation crashing to the ground.'

'When is someone going to come along and sort them out once and for all?' said another statuesque woman with blonde pigtails, a bit stiltedly, almost like she was reading from something. 'How much longer must we live in fear?'

The Parisians around the painting grumbled in agreement.

'This is bad,' said the pirate with a scarf.

The second group of pirates were having a much better time in Madame Tussauds. Over the course of their adventures they had met a great many famous people in the flesh, but they all agreed that meeting famous people in the flesh wasn't all it was cracked up to be, as they tended to be much more boring than you'd hoped, and also shorter. Whereas meeting them in wax form was brilliant, because you could stare at their faces as much as you liked but they couldn't let you down and you could pretend to have a conversation with them in your head where they were witty and erudite.

The pirates stopped in front of a High Seas display.

There was Napoleon and Lord Nelson having an arm wrestle, and Jason and the Argonauts waving from the deck of the *Argo*, and next to that an exciting diorama of Black Bellamy riding atop a big wax squid.

'They've done Black Bellamy very well, haven't they? They've really captured that mischievous gleam in his eye,' said Jennifer.[24]

'But why is it that Black Bellamy has a waxwork when the Pirate Captain doesn't? Is Black Bellamy a more famous pirate?' asked the albino pirate.

'Of course not,' said the pirate in green defensively. 'I'm sure the Captain has been asked to pose, but he probably didn't think wax technology is at a sufficiently high standard to do justice to his air of resolute authority.'

'Do you suppose they have nipples?' the pirate with a peg-leg wondered out loud, trying to peer down Nell Gwyn's top.

'I wonder if they're wax all the way through?'

'Oh, no. They build a frame out of wire, or newspaper, or whatever they have to hand, and then they spray it with a special bee pheromone. That makes all the bees for miles around turn up and cover the frame with wax,' said the pirate who had once been a mailman.

---

24. There is a waxwork museum in Prague that has possibly the least convincing Michael Jackson you could ever hope to see. But it makes up for this with several quite scary golems. Recently, Madame Tussauds in London had to cover up Kylie with a longer skirt because so many visitors were patting her bum it was starting to wear away.

'Really? I didn't know that,' said the albino pirate.

'You see, wax is basically bee sick.'

'What if there aren't any bees about? Bees get all sleepy in winter,' said the pirate who knew a bit about nature.

'Yes, well, in winter they probably use earwax from street urchins instead.'

'Look at me! I'm kissing Charles Babbage!'

'And I'm getting a piggyback from Oliver Cromwell!'

'Ha ha! Marie Antoinette is doing something unspeakable with the Pope!'

They wandered through to the Hall of Crowned Heads, which was supposed to be full of waxworks from all the royal families in Europe, although most of them seemed to be temporarily removed for repairs. The sassy pirate got a match and set about melting the nose of a crowned head who had once tried to trap the pirates down a well.

'Look, here's a waxwork of a dead waxwork-museum curator with a spear coming out of his back,' said the pirate in green. 'They've even done a little pool of wax blood! That's very clever, isn't it?'

The pirates looked at the dead waxwork-museum curator waxwork sprawled across the floor. Jennifer bent down and prodded it.

'I think,' she said, wrinkling her nose, 'that this is an actual dead body.' Even though she was a Victorian lady, she had seen a number of dead bodies since becoming a pirate, and was getting to be quite an expert on the subject, though she had not let this affect her breezy outlook.

'Was it old age?' said the albino pirate hopefully.

'I don't think spears in the back are often a symptom of old age, no.'

'Oh dear.'

'Moider!' said the pirate from the Bronx.

All the pirates jumped with a start as the sound of heavy footsteps echoed down the hallway.

'Somebody's coming!' said the pirate in green.

'Oh! It's bound to be the murderer. They always return to the scene of the crime. And what if they're not done murdering?'

'Quick, we'll pretend to be a piratical diorama.'

'What should we do?' said the albino pirate in a panic. 'What goes on in a piratical diorama?'

'Pirate stuff. You two, pretend to be having a duel,' said Jennifer.

'What about me?' said the pirate in green.

'Pretend to be in the middle of ravishing me.'

'I don't really know what that means,' said the pirate in green, turning crimson. 'We tend to stick to the pillage and plundering part of piracy.'

'Here, grab my dress like this.'

The pirates had just frozen into an exciting diorama when two gigantic statuesque blonde ladies with long blonde pigtails marched into the room.

'Jennifer,' whispered the pirate in green.

'Sssh,' hissed Jennifer.

'What if one of the bees comes and lands on my nose?'

'What are you talking about?'

'The bees that make the wax.'

'Please be quiet.'

'It's just I'm allergic to bees.'

'Shut. Up.'

'Did those pirates in that piratical diorama say something?' said one of the statuesque blonde ladies, peering at Jennifer suspiciously.

The other statuesque blonde lady came across and looked the albino pirate up and down.

'Don't be stupid, Helga,' she said. 'They are wax. Look, this one isn't even particularly realistic.'

The first statuesque blonde lady shrugged, and grabbed a couple of the remaining crowned heads under each arm.

'Oh, this one's heavy.'

'I think that's Poland. It's all the meat in their diet.'

'Is this the last of them?'

'Yes. Let's get them loaded up and be on our way.'

The third group of pirates were sat in the audience of the Folies Bergère. Whilst they weren't having as good a time as the pirates at Madame Tussauds, they were having a better time than the pirates at the Louvre, although they were having to sit through a lot of boring acts that the programme assured them contained biting satire whilst they waited for the dancing girls.

'I heard that when they dance they blow kisses at the men in the audience,' said the pirate with a hook for a hand.

'I heard that they don't wear any knickers when they do the cancan!' said the pirate with rickets.

'I heard that you can see their bare tummies.'

'I heard that they don't wear any knickers when they do the cancan!' said the pirate with rickets.

In the row in front of them sat a small group of Parisian gents, knocking back absinthe and smoking cigars. They were talking about how the Folies Bergère wasn't as popular as it usually was.

'Excuse me,' said the pirate in red, leaning forward, 'I hope you don't mind me asking, but why do you think that is?'

'Peuh!' said one of the Parisians with a Gallic shrug. 'Who can say? Perhaps it is the *Ring Cycle* opera of Monsieur Wagner? It's the talk of the town.'

'But that's on in London,' said the pirate with a hook for a hand.

'Oh, no,' said the Parisian, 'it's on a tour of Europe. It doesn't stay in one place for very long.'

'Like a tramp!' said the pirate with long legs.

'Do tramps sing?'

'Do you remember that adventure when the Pirate Captain decided that he should do something about the homeless and he adopted that tramp? He sang quite a lot if I recall.'

'Especially when he drank all the Captain's grog.'

'Yes. Poor Trampy. I wonder how he's getting on in Antarctica. He looked quite cold when we left him.'

'I heard that they don't wear any knickers when they do the cancan!' said the pirate with rickets.

The pirates waited while yet another comedian went through a routine about relationships. While they *had* always wondered about what was up with women stealing the duvet, they were getting very impatient. Fortunately, the comedian was followed by the cancan dancers, who high-kicked their way on to the stage. The music speeded up. The dancers kicked higher and higher. The pirates craned forward for a better look, in the anticipation of having absolutely nothing left to their imagination.[25]

'Oh,' said the pirate with rickets.

'Oh dear,' said the pirate with long legs.

'That's not what I was expecting at all.'

---

25. The 'cancan' literally translates as 'scandal' or 'tittle-tattle' and first appeared in Paris in 1830.

Eight

AMBUSHED BY KILL-CRAZY LOBSTERS

The three sets of pirates all arrived back at the salon at the same time to find the Pirate Captain stretched out on a chaise longue in the middle of the room holding forth to Marx, Engels and an appreciative-looking audience of Parisian intellectuals. The pirates waited politely for him to finish, because he was clearly in the middle of some important philosophising.

'. . . and that's why, in a straight fight, I think a shark would most likely defeat Dracula,' said the Pirate Captain thoughtfully.

All the Parisian intellectuals clapped their hands. The men nodded and stroked their pointy beards, whilst the ladies fanned themselves and jostled for the Captain's attention.

The Pirate Captain noticed his crew and waved them over. 'Hello, number two,' he said. 'I seem to have become a cause célèbre.'

'Could we have a word, Captain?' asked the pirate with a scarf.

'Of course. Excuse me, gentlemen, ladies. I'll just be a moment.'

'Don't leave us for too long,' said a lady intellectual. 'We are all so keen to hear your views on the nature of consciousness.'

'Oh, that's easy,' said the Captain, with a wink. 'It's little people inside your brain. They're the size of earwigs.'

He strolled over to his pirates, grinning.

'I'm really enjoying this, number two. I've often felt it's a shame my wit and wisdom have been confined to the likes of you lot, when they could be benefiting a much broader audience. Amazing that it took someone like Marx to realise it. So then, what have the rest of you been up to? Anything that might help lead to a proper adventure?'

The pirates all started talking at once.

'We saw the most amazing thing at the Folies Bergère!'

'Not as amazing as what happened at the waxworks!'

'Wait till you hear about what happened at the Louvre!'

The Captain waved for them all to be quiet. Because the pirates often got up to pretty exciting stuff, they frequently had a problem with who wanted to tell their anecdote first. To avoid the situation escalating to bloodshed, a while back the Pirate Captain had drawn up a list of topics for potential anecdotes and, through a complex bit of maths, assigned them various scores. Thus it could quickly be decided which anecdote was best and so deserved to be told first.

The topics were:

- an anecdote featuring a ham. (10 points)
- an anecdote featuring nudity. (7 points)
- an anecdote featuring murder. (5 points)
- an anecdote featuring somebody being eaten by a creature. (4 points)
- an anecdote featuring problems with public transport. (1 point)

'Right,' said the Pirate Captain. 'My anecdote features ham. Do any of your anecdotes feature ham?'

The pirates shook their heads sadly.

'Well then. In addition to spending most of the day impressing high society with my intriguing philosophical debates, I also tried some of that French ham today. It was OK, nothing special. Bit salty.'

'That *is* a good anecdote, Captain,' said the pirate in green.

All the pirates were glad they'd heard the Captain's story first.

'Our anecdote features murder,' said Jennifer. 'We went to the waxworks, and they were really good, especially the mechanical ones that jiggle about like they're dancing. Anyhow, then we found a murdered body. And some mysterious statuesque blonde ladies with pigtails turned up and started stealing the crowned heads of Europe. We had to pretend to be waxworks ourselves, or who knows what they might have done to us.'

'Jennifer was really brave,' added the pirate in green. He wanted to get a bit of 'will-they-won't-they?' speculation going amongst the rest of the crew.

'Well, our anecdote *should* have featured nudity, because we decided to go to the Folies Bergère,' said the pirate with a hook for a hand. 'It was quite exciting, but also melancholy, because the dancing ladies all had that kind of particularly lovely face that just makes you want to cry into your pillow all night. Anyhow, when it came to the finale, which as you know is meant to leave nothing to the imagination, well, they were all wearing big serious-looking bucket pants! Made out of sacks! The crowd all starting booing, but the statuesque Nordic lady with pigtails stood up and told everybody that it was by order of the communists, because communists felt that not wearing any underwear was a bit much.'

'Are we against a lack of pants now? I do lose track a bit,' said Marx.

'No,' said Engels. 'We said that it's all about context. If it's "artistic", then that's OK.'

'The Folies Bergère are French, so they must be artistic,' said the pirate in green.

'Precisely. We'd have no problem with that,' said Engels.

'We went to the Louvre,' said the pirate with a scarf, going next. 'I think we probably drew the short straw, because although we feel culturally enriched, we didn't get to see any murders or high-kicking legs. We got a bit of art theft, which isn't bad, I suppose. Someone had tried to make it look like the communists had stolen the *Mona Lisa*! A hefty blonde was telling all the crowd how terrible it was and how if we had a strong government who weren't afraid to act then we'd soon see the end of the "red reign of terror".'

'It's just like in London!' cried Marx. 'Obviously, somebody is intent on blackening our name. But who could be carrying out such a thing? And for what possible motive?'

'Aaarrrr,' said the Pirate Captain, narrowing his eyes and tapping his chin.

'Oh, good God. He's going to start going on about his "detective skills" again,' muttered the pirate in red, holding his head in his hands.

'In the course of my many adventures,' said the Pirate Captain, taking on an air of authority, 'I've noticed that when sinister dealings are afoot, one is usually looking for a culprit. "Culprit" is a technical term for somebody who is up to no good. It's usually the last person you suspect. Like a pillar of the community. Or a kindly spinster. Have you noticed any pillars of the community or kindly spinsters skulking about?'

'Afraid not, Captain.'

'Well, not to worry. As I may have mentioned before, I'm a bit of an expert when it comes to solving mysteries and criminal matters. For instance, did you know that nine times out of ten you can discover who the guilty party is simply by comparing the butt of a cigarette left at the crime scene with the brand he smokes?'

'Except we didn't find any cigarette butts, Captain.'

'Really? That's unusual.' The Pirate Captain clicked his tongue thoughtfully. 'We're clearly dealing with a professional. In which case, the identity of the criminal is usually given away by a dog failing to bark, thereby revealing the fact that the intruder was familiar to the victim. Case closed.'

'Not sure that really helps either, Captain,' said the pirate in green. 'Because we didn't see any dogs.'

'Then it seems,' said the Captain, holding up a finger dramatically, 'that the villain was a jellyfish all along!'

'Actually, Captain,' said the pirate in red, with a world-weary sigh, 'the keen observer will notice a common thread. Something all these stories have in common.'

'All the stories are about pirates!' shouted the albino pirate excitedly.

'Besides that. All the stories feature these mysterious statuesque blonde women.'

The Pirate Captain frowned, and tried to remember something important. Unfortunately, the years of drinking grog mixed with gunpowder had left the 'remembering things' part of the Captain's brain a bit shot, though the 'knowing a lot about meat' part of his brain had done its best to compensate for this. He screwed up his eyes in concentration. He did his best not to think about hams. He thought about the mysterious blonde ladies. Then he thought about how sad it was that ladies weren't very good at growing luxuriant beards. He wondered if perhaps that could be a motive, because maybe they were jealous of Marx's facial hair. Then he thought about how much better his own beard was compared to Marx's, which led him on to thinking about how oak-like his broad neck was. That made him think about how fantastic he looked in his nice new coat. And then he sat bolt upright.

'Eureka!' he cried, and he pointed at his coat as if by way of explanation. Marx and the pirates looked at him blankly. 'Valkyries! Viking mania! The opera! From what I've heard, operas nowadays are stuffed full of hefty statuesque blonde ladies.'

'And the opera was in London when we were suffering mishaps there, and now it's here, where our troubles have followed us, which is more than a little suspicious,' exclaimed Engels.

'That's what operas do. They move about. They're like tramps, you see,' said the albino pirate knowledgeably.

Marx called over a waitress and asked for a copy of the day's newspaper. They turned quickly to the 'What's On' section.

WAGNER'S OPERA GALA PERFORMANCE
TONIGHT

CHAMPAGNE RECEPTION
FOR THE CROWNED
HEADS OF EUROPE

MAGIC RINGS,
GOBLINS AND THAT

LADIES MAY GET THE
VAPOURS

The Pirate Captain looked up from the newspaper with a gleam in his eye. Gleams in the Pirate Captain's eye could be mainly split into three groups: gleams caused by his eyeball reflecting some sort of treasure, gleams caused by the unhealthy amount of copper in his diet and gleams caused by his spying an opportunity to put on a disguise.

'Well then,' he said. 'There's only one thing for it. I shall have to disguise myself as a crowned head and use my natural charm to win the confidence of this Wagner chap. It won't be easy. And obviously I'll miss your company as I chomp on those little canapés made from wafer-thin beef. But you know me – I don't think twice before putting myself in the path of danger by talking to sultry princesses about court gossip.'

The pirates all marvelled at the sacrifices that their Captain was willing to make. They made a collective mental note to describe him as 'magnanimous' in the future.

'Pirate Captain,' said Marx, 'I feel responsible for putting you in this position. I'm coming with you.'

'Yes, why not? You can be my butler. And Jennifer can be a lady-in-waiting. It's important to show I've got a staff.'

'Can't I be another crowned head?' said Marx, with a bit of a pout. 'I'm not being a butler. Butlering goes against all my principles.'

'Oh, this sort of thing happens on all our adventures,' replied the Captain, grinning again. 'You say something like "I'd rather die than wear that butler suit", and before you know it, we're being announced in the ballroom of this opera house with you in a butler suit.'

'There's no way you're getting me in that butler suit,' said Marx.

Nine

THE SPOON-WORM
FURY

'His Royal Imperial Excellency the Crowned Head of Bootyopia,' announced a statuesque blonde. 'And his elderly butler, Carruthers.'

The Pirate Captain smiled a dazzling smile at the assorted crowned heads who were milling about at the opera's champagne reception. He waved a little flag that he'd designed himself and puffed out his chest to show off the six rows of gleaming medals he had pinned to his coat. The pirate with long legs had suggested that he should go a bit easier on the latter, but the Pirate Captain said that he didn't want some other crowned head outdoing him on the medal front.

'I can't believe I'm wearing this butler suit,' said Marx.

'It looks very fetching,' said Jennifer encouragingly, doing a little curtsey to a passing prince.

The Pirate Captain waved regally, then chanced a few winks and a bit of pointing to show how at ease he was in such exalted company. The room was a throng of blue-blooded lubbers from all across Europe. Most of the conversation seemed to be about the difficulties of running a big castle, how fun it was riding about in gold carriages and how good congenital blood diseases were.

'Hello, I don't think I've met you,' said a cheerful-looking crowned head, bounding up to the Captain. It said 'Poland' on his sash. 'Bootyopia. Where is that exactly? Is it one of those Baltic ones? Or is it in the middle where all those mountains are?'

'Yes, that's it. Around those parts,' said the Pirate Captain vaguely.

'Unusual name, Bootyopia.'

'It's like Ethiopia, but with "Booty" rather than "Ethi",' the Captain explained. 'It's named after the fact that we have more treasure per capita than any other country.'

'I like your flag.'

'You see.' The Pirate Captain shot Marx a triumphant look. 'My butler has been saying it's too cluttered.'

'Oh, no, not at all,' said Poland. 'I especially like the lamb jumping over the boat. Do you actually have lambs that size in Bootyopia, or is it some sort of metaphor?'[26]

26. Libya probably has the most boring flag of any country: a green rectangle with no insignia. The biggest flag in the world is flown in the capital of Brazil, and weighs 600 kg, as much as two fat manatees.

'They're actually that big. You get the most amazing chops out of them.'

'Incredible. We only have normal-sized lambs, although we do have a lot of meat in our diet. That's why we're so heavy compared to other people,' said Poland. 'Do you export them? The lambs?'

'No, mostly we're famous for the export of our beards and our women. We're said to have the glossiest beards and women in the whole of Europe. Have you seen my medals? I've got twenty-eight.' The Pirate Captain pointed to his medals.

'Oh, yes. Very nice. I've got twenty-three,' said Poland.

'This one is for fighting. This one is for fighting too. This one is for when Bootyopia won the Eurovision Song Contest. And this one is actually for when I won "Best In Breed" at Crufts. Heads up! Canapés.'[27]

'So,' said Engels, looking at the salon's clock and helping himself to another croissant, 'do you think they'll need rescuing yet?'

The pirate with a scarf shrugged. 'I tend to give the Captain at least an hour to get himself into trouble. Maybe a bit longer if he's got Jennifer with him.'

---

27. On attending the Bayreuth Opera Festival, Tchaikovsky remarked: 'Cutlets, baked potatoes and omelettes – all are discussed much more eagerly than Wagner's music.'

'Really? That's pretty good. I usually only give Marx about twenty minutes.'

They both watched a couple of pirates who were sat in the corner seeing if they could fit an entire copy of Voltaire's *Dictionnaire philosophique* in their mouths.

'I'm sure they'll be fine. Though the Pirate Captain does have a bit of a tendency to forget what he was in the middle of and start doing something else entirely. But like he's always saying, it's part of his charm.' The pirate with a scarf paused and looked a bit rueful. 'There's a lot of stuff like that that's "part of his charm".'

'Do you ever get frustrated with being a sidekick?' asked Engels glumly. 'Because I have to say, I'm starting to find it a little tiresome.'

'Well, there's not a whole lot of glory in the sidekick line of work,' agreed the pirate with a scarf. 'But that's not what it's about, is it? And besides, we're in good company. All sorts of important historical characters have had sidekicks.'

'Like who?' said Engels with a frown.

'Well, there's Jesus. He had that friendly ghost version of himself. And Ulysses. He had that minotaur he rode about on. And, um, Hannibal. I think he had a talking elephant . . .'

'Excuse me,' said a lady intellectual, coming and sitting down next to them. 'Do you know if your philosopher-pirate man will be gone long? It's just that he promised to show me his moral compass, and I'm very excited by the prospect.'

'He's off solving a mystery at the opera house, I'm afraid,' explained the pirate with a scarf politely.

The lady intellectual looked stricken. 'Goodness! But I have heard such terrible things about the opera!'

'Yes, it is meant to go on a bit,' agreed the pirate with a scarf. 'But I wouldn't worry, because the Pirate Captain is quite good at keeping himself occupied. He makes up little shanties about creatures. I actually think he's at his happiest when he's doing that.'

'No, young man,' said the lady intellectual, 'I was referring to these awful rumours.'

'Rumours?'

'Have you not heard?' The lady intellectual leant forward and continued in a conspiratorial whisper: 'They say that the opera is haunted! Everywhere it goes, there is always one box reserved for a mysterious man. Hardly anybody has ever laid eyes on him. But apparently he's a giant. Enveloped in smoke. Like a demon! My friend Evangeline was telling me the fiend breathes actual fire and has hands the size of suckling pigs. But then again, Evangeline talks a lot of rot, so you never know.'

Engels and the pirate with a scarf gave each other a worried look.

'I do hope nothing evil befalls your captain,' added the lady intellectual. 'He has such nice shiny boots.'

The Pirate Captain was enjoying being a crowned head almost as much as being a philosopher. 'At the moment, Bootyopia is a parliamentary democracy, which to be quite honest is a bit of a bore,' he explained to a gaggle of other crowned heads. 'Apparently it's considered unfair to cut a fellow's head off on a whim. Ridiculous. But there are advantages, because with my role primarily as a figurehead, I have more time to mooch about the palace and pose for tapestries and the like.'

'What about your national anthem?' asked the Crowned Head of Prussia. 'For some reason, I can't seem to think how the Bootyopian anthem goes.'

'Funny you should mention that,' said the Pirate Captain. 'I'm actually here to ask that Wagner fellow about writing me a new one. Something that reflects what a modern, thrusting state Bootyopia is – you know, something with a bit of a beat. Which one is he again?'

The Crowned Head of Spain got his butler to point towards where the composer was holding forth. He wasn't much to look at. If the rest of the pirates had been there, they would probably have compared him to one of the more spidery fonts, like *Monotype Corsiva*. A pirate with a lot of experience in describing mouths would confidently say that Wagner's mouth was 'sucked in' and had sardonic lips around it. The mouth-describer's friend, who was good at describing chins, would say that Wagner's chin was 'wilful' and 'pointed'. Above both of these features was a pair of piercing blue eyes, which needed no further description.

'. . . The idea came to me in a dream,' Wagner was saying. 'Mighty Thor appeared. He showed me the score for the greatest opera ever to grace the stage. It deals with important topical issues, such as "All midgets are untrustworthy, pitiful and loathsome" and "Women are teasing, meddling, capricious and mainly interested in gold". It touches on betrayal and love and man's struggle to realise everything he can be. All through the medium of bears, volcanoes, dragons and magic swords. I was shown all this, and then Thor said I was brilliant and flew off.'

'Funny things, dreams,' said the Captain, slipping expertly into the conversation. 'I've got a book somewhere that tells you all about their hidden meanings. For instance, I have a recurring dream where I'm on a dark country lane, and I'm trying to run from something, but I can't move my legs, as if they're trapped in treacle. Then all my teeth fall out, and I realise I'm naked. I think it means I'm going to come into money.'

'Sorry,' said Wagner, 'I don't think we've been introduced.'

'I,' said the Pirate Captain, 'am His Royal Majesty the King of Bootyopia, Terror of the High Seas.'

'Terror of the High Seas?' repeated Wagner quizzically.

'Aaarrrr, yes. Because we do a lot of polluting.' The Captain made a mental note to remember to change his catchphrase along with his disguise. 'I feel quite guilty about it, really. But anyhow, I just wanted to say that I used to think opera was a terrible waste of time and effort, but you've won me round with this *Ring Cycle* of yours.'

'That's very kind of you,' said Wagner. 'Can I ask which bits of my operas are your favourite?'

The Pirate Captain puffed out a lungful of air. 'Difficult to say, there's so much of it that I like. Let me see. The instruments are good. What are those big ones, like a trumpet but bigger?'

'Tubas?'

'That's it! Tubas. I love the tuba bits. Parumpum-pum-um! Brilliant stuff.'

'I don't think I've ever used tubas, Your Excellency,' said Wagner. 'I find them rather too bombastic and exciting.'

'When I said "tubas", I mean "the bits where you stick it to those filthy communists". Because I hate communists,' said the Pirate Captain.

'Really, Your Excellency?' said Wagner, fixing him with a stare.

'Oh, yes. For example, if this butler of mine turned out to be a communist, I'd have him drowned in honey and then fed to stoats in the traditional Bootyopian fashion.'

Marx looked a little uneasy. The Captain gave him a cuff round the ear for effect.

'The only thing that worries me,' the Pirate Captain went on in a conspiratorial whisper, 'is that nobody seems to be conducting a diabolical Europe-wide scheme to discredit the communists and create a general panic about them. Why, if someone was doing that, I'd probably give him a big chunk of Bootyopia and fund any operas he wanted to put on. No matter how boring they were. Assuming this person was an opera composer, that is.'

Wagner looked the Pirate Captain and Marx up and down. The Pirate Captain winked, flicked a speck of imaginary dust from one of his epaulettes and adjusted some of his medals. Just as he was starting to think he'd been too subtle, Wagner smiled.

'Well, Your Excellency. I think we should talk. Perhaps I could give you a tour?'

'That sounds delightful,' said the Captain, winking again, this time with both eyes at once.

Ten

ON THE ISLAND OF
LOVE-STARVED
JELLYFISH

Engels and the pirates hurried down to the opera house, though not so fast that they got a stitch. There was some debate about what the best way of getting into the opera would be. Some of the pirates suggested disguising themselves as moles and burrowing their way in. Some of them suggested putting mushrooms on the wall and waiting for it to rot away. A few of them suggested blocking out the moon, though they were a bit vague about how this would help. But eventually, Engels pointed out that seeing as it was an opera, perhaps the easiest way to get in would simply be to buy tickets. When they arrived at the box office, the pirate with a scarf, always keen to take care of the boat's finances, got some of the pirates to walk on their knees, so that they only had to pay children's prices, and he made sure he got a discount for the pirates who had eyes or bits of limb missing.

'You've no idea how hard it was to get hold of the bears,' said Wagner, as he led Marx, Jennifer and the Pirate Captain through the bowels of the opera house, 'for the scene set in the dragon's forest. You can't have an enchanted forest without bears.'

'Can they sing?' asked the Pirate Captain.

Wagner pulled a face. 'No. We tried training them. Like all bears, they love dancing, but we can't get them to sing more than "Arooo" and "Rarrgh". It's a shame.'

The Pirate Captain couldn't help but agree. He'd spent many a happy evening with the crew debating what a bear would sound like if it could sing. And at the back of his mind, he had a good idea that before long he'd be facing some sort of terrible peril, and it would go down a lot easier if there was a chorus of bears singing away in the background.

'In Bootyopia, pigeons have taken the ecological niche of bears,' the Captain started, but Wagner groaned and held up a hand to cut him off.

'If you tell me one more thing about Bootyopia,' he said, rubbing his temple wearily, 'I'm going to pull out my own eyebrows. There isn't a Bootyopia. You're not the Crowned Head of Bootyopia. And this isn't your harmless old butler. You're the Pirate Captain, and this is the communist Karl Marx. I don't know who the young lady is, but I must say she has lovely cheekbones.'

Jennifer beamed. The Pirate Captain always felt that the best way to deal with difficult situations like this was just to plough on regardless and pretend nobody had said anything untoward.

'So, another interesting fact about Bootyopia is that we have the lowest average precipitation of any—'

'Captain!' exclaimed Wagner.

The Pirate Captain pouted. 'How did you know?'

'It wasn't very difficult,' explained Wagner. 'Marx's disguise is pretty good – he has that sort of servile look about him anyway. But, Pirate Captain, your boots – not only are they emblazoned with anchors and the like, but they also have "Pirate Captain" written around the edges.'

'Damn my vanity,' said the Pirate Captain, nodding.

'And the piratical roaring that peppers your conversation. That's a bit of a giveaway.'

'Damn the irrepressible pirate blood that runs in my veins!'

'And the big skull and crossbones on your hat, which is, incidentally, a pirate's hat.'

'Damn my reluctance to take off my pirate hat!'

ʒ

The rest of the pirates spent so long trying to decide if it was best to have salted popcorn on top of sugared popcorn or the other way round that the opera had already started by the time they made it into the auditorium. They did their best to stop their buckles and cutlasses rattling as they tiptoed to their seats.

Up on stage, next to a gigantic and menacing-looking volcano, a hefty, statuesque blonde was singing about how terrible the liberal bias in the media was these days. The key theme of the opera seemed to be how feelings made people soft and useless. To make the point clearer, Wagner had incorporated several characters dressed in tabards labelled with 'Being Sad', 'Staring At a Sunset', 'Cooing Over Babies' and other feelings, who were now being chased about by bears.

'These opera glasses are good,' said the pirate with a nut allergy, peering into the albino pirate's ear. 'I think I can see your brain.'

'According to this,' said the pirate in green, reading from his programme, 'everything has its own musical theme. There's a theme for the volcano and a theme for the bears and so on. Isn't that clever? We should adopt something like that for when we're on the pirate boat.'

'If the Pirate Captain had a theme, how do you think it would go?' said the albino pirate.

'Oh, it would be lilting,' said the pirate in green, 'but at the same time have drums and things, because you'd have to show his myriad depths.'

'This is definitely our most cultural adventure yet,' said the pirate with gout.

'Right, tell us what's going on, you rogue, or I'll slice your gizzard open,' said the Pirate Captain, deciding to take the more direct approach, and waggling his cutlass at Wagner's wilful chin. 'Bear in mind that I don't even know what a gizzard is – so it would be a pretty messy exercise while I tried to find out.' The Captain did his best piratical glower. 'We were discussing the subject earlier, and Marx still thinks this is all something to do with his beard; whereas I'm convinced you're his long-lost brother gone evil. So which is it?'

Wagner sighed. 'Please, Pirate Captain, I am an innocent party in all of this. You must believe me. There is something unnatural here. I am beset by a demon! Something not of this world.'

'Piffle!' exclaimed Marx. 'You're not scaring us off with ghost stories.'

Wagner looked miserably at his shoes. 'It all started some months ago,' he explained. 'I received a strange anonymous letter from somebody who claimed to be my biggest fan. He offered to become my benefactor. At first

I was delighted. He asked for a private box at wherever we should be touring to, but nothing more. I thought it was maybe a little odd that he would only communicate by leaving me notes, but I didn't pay it too much mind – I simply assumed he wanted to preserve his anonymity. But the notes became more and more demanding. He brought in his own staff. He wanted changes made to my work. The truth is, I've grown tired of goblins and magic swords. It all seems rather childish now. My real ambition is to write light-hearted comedies, ones where people fall out of cupboards and vicars are always coming round for tea at awkward moments. But he was having none of it. And I fear that now my whole opera is being used for devilish purposes.'

'So you've never even seen this benefactor of yours?'

'Just once. But it was dark.' Wagner looked momentarily terrified. 'And he had such a countenance as I cannot describe.'

'A countenance like a wolf?' suggested Marx.

'No, not really like a wolf.'

'A countenance like a zombie?' suggested Jennifer.

'No, not much like a zombie either.'

'A countenance like a fish?' suggested the Pirate Captain.

'Well, shiny like a fish. So, yes, that's probably closest. But bigger, a veritable giant. And shrouded in smoke, with the glowing eyes of a demon. That's not just me using poetic language, he really looked like that.'

They stopped outside the entrance to an opera box. 'Here it is,' said Wagner, dabbing some sweat from his temple with a handkerchief. 'The phantom's secret box.'

'You know,' said the Captain, 'I keep a box in my office onboard the pirate boat. I wrote "Top Secret!" on the side, and I warn the men to never go near it. In actual fact, all that's in the thing is a pepper pot I made at school and a couple of nice pebbles I found on Brighton beach. But it drives the lads crazy. This glowing-eyed demon fellow is probably up to the same thing, but on a slightly bigger scale. Trying to give himself an enigmatic air of mystery.'

'I suppose that might be all there is to it,' said Wagner doubtfully. He looked at his pocket watch and gasped. 'I must return to the performance, or he will know something is amiss.' He cast a desperate gaze at the Pirate Captain. 'Do you think you can rid me of this demon?'

'Well, as something of an expert on this kind of phenomena, I have to say it all depends on the type of demon,' said the Captain, with a shrug. 'For instance, if it turns out that the opera house was built on the sight of an old Indian burial ground, then that could spell trouble. They're the worst kind of ghostly phantasm, Red Indians, because when they kill you they don't let any part of your anatomy go to waste, on account of them caring so much about their environment. I don't fancy eldritch spirits using my hands as bookends or something. But we'll do our best.'

Wagner shook his hand gratefully, bowed to Marx and Jennifer and then hared off down the corridor.

The trio crept inside. It was quite cluttered for an opera box – there was a wardrobe, and a table, and piles of books, as if somebody very untidy had been living there. It certainly lacked a woman's touch. Some flickering candles cast spooky shadows across the walls, which were made even more spooky by the Pirate Captain doing shadow shapes of dinosaurs with his hands.

'That's really not helping,' said Jennifer.

'Sorry. Bit on the creepy side, all this.'

'You don't actually believe the culprit to be some kind of beast from the netherworld?' asked Marx. 'It's balderdash. Superstitious mumbo-jumbo. There's no such thing as giant glowering-eyed demons. What Wagner saw was probably just a trick of the light, or a weather balloon.'

'Well, talking about it isn't going to help,' said Jennifer briskly. 'We should search for clues.'

'Yes, I suppose you're right,' said Marx, looking around. He frowned. 'What does a clue look like?'

'Hard to say. That's the trouble with clues. They can be all sorts. Hastily scrawled notes. A tell-tale piece of fabric left on a rusty nail. In this case it's probably a file marked top secret, or some sort of plan.'

'Where would *you* keep a plan?' asked Marx, still at a bit of a loss.

'Probably in a special drawer, or a nice new lever-arch file, something like that. We once had an adventure with a city council who wanted to build over protected fenland, and their plan was tattooed on the backs of a pair of twins who had been separated at birth.'

'Have you found any twins who have been separated at birth yet?' said Marx hopefully.

'Not yet,' said the Pirate Captain.

'A secret diary would be good too. They're a fantastic source of clues. Except of course you shouldn't really read other people's diaries, because it's extremely impolite.'

All of a sudden Marx froze. 'Look there!' he hissed, the blood draining from his face. 'There's somebody *watching us from that wardrobe!*'

He pointed to the corner of the opera box where a huge wooden wardrobe stood, its door slightly ajar. In the gloom it was just possible to see a pair of gimlet eyes peering out at them.

'What are they doing?' asked Jennifer.

'They're just . . . staring. Staring with cold, dead eyes,' whispered Marx.

'Psychotic eyes! The kind of eyes that wouldn't blink as they sliced you open!' added the Pirate Captain, ducking behind him.

'Oh, for goodness' sakes!' said Jennifer. She pushed past them, marched up to the wardrobe door and smartly yanked the door open. 'Get out of there,' she commanded.

The Crowned Head of Spain fell out on to the floor with a waxy *thud*.

'Aha,' said Marx, wiping his brow in relief. 'So that's what's happened to the waxworks.' Sure enough, the wardrobe was piled high with all the stolen crowned heads of Europe.

'Well done, Jennifer,' said the Pirate Captain, trying to make it look like he'd actually been tying his shoelace rather than ducking in fright. 'That was admirably feisty.'

'Not really,' said Jennifer, giving him a bit of a look. 'I've spent enough time on the pirate boat to get used to dealing with peeping Toms.'

The Pirate Captain stared guiltily at the floor, whistled a little tune and went back to busying himself with fascinating clue-hunting.

'How about this?' Marx indicated a big model town sat atop a desk. 'Do you think this could be a clue?'

'Yes, that's almost certainly a clue, though I'm not sure what it means,' said Jennifer.

'Oh, this is brilliant,' said the Pirate Captain happily. 'You see, this is what I like about those villainous ne'er-do-well types. They always have stuff like this. Before I was going to be a pirate, I was going to be an architect. Mainly because I really, *really* like these kinds of models. I wonder if it lights up? Oh, look! They've even done little people doing marches. Fantastic.'

'If you stand right next to it, it makes you look enormous!' grinned Marx.

'I'm King Kong!' said the Pirate Captain.

'I'm Gulliver!' said Marx.

Marx and the Pirate Captain were so busy pretending to be giants that it wasn't until Jennifer let out a gasp that they noticed a billowing cloud of diabolical fog rolling through the door.

Eleven

SPONGE MADNESS

'Hell's bells,' said the Captain, ducking behind the desk. 'It looks like a mysterious fog has been the villain all along!' He jabbed his cutlass a bit pointlessly in the direction of the fog. 'Which is a nuisance, because they're notoriously difficult to fight, clouds of mysterious fog. On account of them being incorporeal and that. I have to say, if it was going to be something supernatural, I was hoping for a vampire, because they're a doddle. Stakes, garlic, holy water, true faith, sunlight, fire . . . I'm not sure there's anything that *doesn't* kill a vampire.'

There was an ominous clanking sound from the depths of the billowing fog. Then a foot appeared, and then a leg. Then a big metal head. Eventually, an entire colossal mechanical man stepped forward, and they could now see that the fog wasn't a supernatural miasma, but steam coming out of great big pipes stuck on the mechanical man's back. He was so huge he had to bend down slightly just to fit through the door.

'Aaaarrr,' said the Captain, thinking fast and pulling Marx and Jennifer, who had momentarily frozen, dumbfounded, down behind the desk with him. 'Don't worry, it's not the first time I've encountered a mechanical man. The trick is to pose them an unsolvable logic puzzle. They can't stand that sort of thing. Makes all the cogs in their metal brain get stuck, and then their head falls off.'

'Do you know any logic puzzles?' whispered Marx.

The Captain paused for a moment. 'There's a farmer with a boat. And he's got a fox and a chicken and a sack of grain. Then some stuff happens which I forget. I think the answer is that the farmer has to make a nice pie out of them.'

'Excuse me,' boomed the gigantic mechanical man, with a polite metallic cough. 'It's just I know you're hiding behind the desk, because I can see the peak of your pirate hat.'

The Captain sighed. 'Damn my—'

'Oh, don't start all that again,' said Jennifer, getting to her feet. Marx and the Pirate Captain reluctantly stood up as well.

'Hello there,' said the Pirate Captain for want of anything better to say. 'I'm the Pirate Captain, the one from the newspapers. This is Jennifer, a lady. And this is Karl Marx. He's the leader of the angry urban proletariat.'

'Yes, I know,' said the tin man. 'We've met.' His metal face couldn't really convey expressions, but there was a frosty note to his metallic voice.

'Really?' said Marx. 'I'm sure you're right, but I'm terrible with names.'

The tin man struck a clumsy sort of pose, with his legs apart and his hands on his hips.

'Soon everybody will know the name of Friedrich Nietzsche!' he announced dramatically.

'Oh dear,' the Captain muttered to Marx. 'In my experience, it's never a good sign when they start talking about themselves in the third person.' He turned to the mechanical man. 'You know, boasting really isn't a very attractive quality in a person.'

'Little Fred Nietzsche?' said Marx, looking the mechanical man up and down in surprise. 'Goodness me, you've grown! And there's something else. Have you changed your hair?'

'No,' said the big metal man, sounding a bit peeved. 'I've built myself this fantastic metal body.'

'Oh, yes, that's probably it.' Marx turned to Jennifer and the Pirate Captain. 'Friedrich here used to hang around the intellectual salons. He wrote a sort of philosophy fanzine, which as I recall, was full of slightly creepy fan fiction about Spinoza having secret romantic trysts with Descartes. I'm afraid none of us took him very seriously.'

'Well, I hope you've learnt an important lesson about not squashing young talent,' said the Pirate Captain. 'Because this is what happens: years later you get menaced by colossal mechanical men. I think it's what Buddhists call "coming back to bite you in the ass".' The Captain turned to Nietzsche. 'So you're a philosopher too?'

'I certainly am,' said the mechanical man, sounding very pleased with himself. 'I've come up with a brand-new philosophy all of my own. It's called "Fascism". And it knocks Communism into a cocked hat.'[28]

'I like your little town, by the way,' said the Captain.

'Thank you,' said Nietzsche. 'It's a model of London as it will look once it has become my new capital city. You'll see that I've replaced all the hospitals and schools with opera houses. And the buildings have been designed with tiny windows and lots of concrete, to encourage a general feeling of ennui and despair amongst the populace. Also, I've painted St Paul's Cathedral jet black.'

'That's very clever how you've done the grass. Is that the same stuff they have in greengrocers?'

---

28. Philosophers don't just war with words. In 1946 Ludwig Wittgenstein reportedly chased Karl Popper round a Cambridge common room with a poker, in a dispute over whether there can be such a thing as a philosophical problem.

'It is, yes,' said Nietzsche.

'Getting back to the point,' frowned Jennifer, knowing that the Captain could go off on this tangent for some time. 'Could we ask what all this is about?'

Nietzsche billowed a cloud of steam and looked into the middle distance. 'It's true, I was that poor boy snubbed by the uncaring intelligentsia. But I had what they call an epiphany.'

'I had one of those once,' said the Pirate Captain brightly. 'It was about five years ago. A perfectly normal day. I was just there in my hammock, not getting up to much. And then, right out of the blue, I thought, *What's stopping me having ham for dinner as well as lunch?* I haven't looked back since.'

'My epiphany was better,' said the tin man a bit petulantly. 'I realised that humanity is weak and stupid, like . . .' The colossal tin Nietzsche paused, looking for the right comparison.

'Like goats?' suggested the Captain.

'That's it, like goats. And what goats need is someone to rule over them with a tin fist!'

Marx huffed. 'Rubbish. Goats need socialised medicine and shorter working hours.'

'Surely goats actually just need a goatherd to feed them goat food and keep wolves away?' said the Pirate Captain. 'And maybe one of those little bells so you know if it's wandered off somewhere it shouldn't.'

'That's only what a weak and stupid goat *thinks* it needs. Actually, goats need a strong leader who treats them with the contempt they deserve – a superman. An *übermensch*!' He let out another big gout of steam and stomped his feet for effect. 'And here I am, the first of those *übermensch*. Superior in every way!'[29]

'What actual ways?' asked Marx, puzzled.

The mechanical man looked stumped for a moment. 'Oh, you know. All sorts. I'm better at making clanking sounds. I'm much shinier than I was before. And, um, my tin hide is able to withstand temperatures of 449.47 degrees Fahrenheit.'

'Those hands look a bit clumsy, though.'

'Yes, well, superior in every way, except picking up pencils, or tying shoelaces.'

'And you've been making Dr Marx get the blame for drowning kittens and all that sort of thing so people would get so terrified of Communism they'd think they needed a big iron goatherd to protect them!' fumed Jennifer. 'It's very rude.'

The colossal tin Nietzsche looked guiltily at where his fingernails would have been if he'd had fingernails. 'Yes, that's pretty much it. I needed a bogeyman, and you communists just happened to be about. It wasn't

---

29. Nietzsche introduced the concept of the superman in his book Thus Spoke Zarathustra. DC Comics introduced the concept of 'Krypto the Superdog' in *Adventure Comics* #210 (1955). This is just one of the many reasons why Marvel are better than DC.

really anything personal. It could just as easily have been single mothers, or immigrants, or something like that.'

'Or a spider with a baby's face!' said the Pirate Captain. 'That would have been pretty terrifying.'

'Yes, that would have done very well,' said the colossal tin Nietzsche.

'It's all been very inconvenient,' said Marx, waggling an admonishing finger. 'And I still don't understand the whole business with stealing the waxwork crowned heads. Is it to play practical jokes? You know, leaving them in people's beds and that sort of thing?'

'That's not the *main* reason,' said Nietzsche, fighting back a tinny grin. He did his dramatic voice again. 'For you see, soon every throne in Europe will be occupied by a waxwork!'

'But then the crowned heads won't have anywhere to sit,' pointed out the Pirate Captain.

'No, Pirate Captain. I intend to replace the actual crowned heads of Europe with my waxworks.'

'I'm not sure they'll be keen on the idea.'

'I imagine not. But that's academic, because at the unexpected climax of the opera tonight, a replica volcano will erupt, flooding the auditorium with magma and thereby boiling all the crowned heads into oblivion.'

Nietzsche rummaged about in his desk and held up a helpful visual aid.

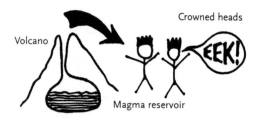

'You see? It's real magma, you know, imported from Italy,' he added proudly. 'Very soon I shall control every nation in Europe, with my puppet governments spreading my philosophy far and wide, and me pulling the strings, like a huge gleaming puppeteer. I did think about making actual puppets, but in the end I decided the waxworks would be less bother. That's the great thing about crowned heads – they don't actually have to do anything, just stand around looking expensive, and nobody will realise anything is amiss.'

'Well, it's all very ingenious,' said the Pirate Captain. 'But I'm afraid you've been forgetting your *one terrible weakness!*' And with that, the Pirate Captain triumphantly whipped out his ship's compass. 'Now what are you going to do? My magnetic compass will scramble your tin brain.' He sprinted forward, clambered daringly up Nietzsche's arm and pressed the compass against his metal forehead.[30]

---

30. In September 2005 pirates attacked a vessel en route to Singapore that was carrying 660 tonnes of tin, worth $4.7 million. A month later the ship was found sunk, with the cargo still onboard, probably because the pirates realised tin makes for rubbish bendy cutlasses.

The colossal tin Nietzsche hefted a weary sigh. 'I'm not sure I know where to begin. For a start, your compass is tiny. And it doesn't contain a magnet. Also, tin isn't magnetic.'

'Aarrrr,' said the Pirate Captain, feeling a little ridiculous now, perched on the giant's shoulder like a big version of Gary, the ship's parrot. 'So,' he added, 'there's this farmer with a wolf and a chicken and—' But before he could get any further a swat from Nietzsche's big tin hand sent the Captain sailing through the air. Luckily, his fall was broken by the model city. And luckier still, he landed on Hyde Park rather than the Houses of Parliament or one of London's pointier landmarks. There was a crunching sound, and the whole of London cracked down the middle and collapsed.

'My model town!' wailed Nietzsche, holding his hands up to his head in frustration. 'Two years that took me to build. Two years!' He bent his metal legs and kneeled on the floor. 'You've ruined it, you clumsy oaf!' A single drop of oil rolled from one of his eyes.

The Pirate Captain picked a few bits of Marble Arch out of his beard, fought back the urge to apologise, and whilst Nietzsche was preoccupied cradling the remains of Buckingham Palace, he, Marx and Jennifer bolted from the room. They charged down the stairs, with the Captain leading the way, but because he didn't have time to consult the tattoos on his feet telling him which direction was left and which direction was right, they were pretty quickly lost in the opera's maze of corridors. The trio paused, panting, as a steady clanking sound grew closer.

'I think we've upset him,' said Marx.

'The Captain does rather seem to have that effect on people,' said Jennifer.

'Quickly! Through this door!' said the Pirate Captain.

Twelve

EEL STAMPEDE!

During his long career and many adventures, the Pirate Captain had often found himself saying, 'Quickly! Through this door!' In the past, saying, 'Quickly! Through this door!' had variously led to: a room full of scorpions; a nest of killer African bees; the ceremonial chamber of a sinister cabal of Satanists; and a pit of stinging nettles. Saying 'Quickly! Through this door!' had never yet led to: a stable full of fast horses; a useful cupboard of muskets; a pile of ham; or the shower room of a young women's tennis club.

This time, 'Quickly! Through this door!' resulted in the three of them tumbling straight on to the opera stage. The huge replica volcano bubbled malevolently away just in front of them. The Captain decided it might be time he gave serious consideration to using some other phrase, seeing as he seemed to be having such poor results with his current effort.

'Funny sort of smell,' said Marx, frowning. 'Like some sort of creature.'

'Bush babies? Sloths? Slow lorises?' said the Captain hopefully.

'More like bear,' said Jennifer, pointing to a group of bears who were lumbering across the stage towards them.

'Oh dear. I'm not very keen on bears,' said Marx. 'I have an irrational fear that they'll rip me to shreds.'

The trio made to turn back the way they'd come, but there, waiting ominously in the wings, stood Nietzsche. He waved at them, and then he drew a big metal finger across his throat, which the Pirate Captain was pretty sure wasn't supposed to signify anything good.

'Right,' said the Captain, taking charge. 'Up the volcano. We'll be safe there because bears can't climb things. It's something to do with the shape of their shoulders.'

They started to clamber up the side of the replica volcano.

'Goodness me,' said the Captain, 'the workmanship that's gone into this thing is very impressive.'

'Cold comfort, Pirate Captain.'

'No, but really. It must have taken him *ages*.'

There was a snuffling sound, and he looked back to see the bears gamely following them up the volcano.

'Actually,' said the Pirate Captain. 'It might be sharks that can't climb things.'

'Look! It's the Pirate Captain! I didn't even know he was in the opera!' said the pirate with gout happily, peering through his opera glasses. He waved. 'Yoo hoo! Pirate Captain!'

'I'm confused,' said the Crowned Head of Bulgaria, leaning across to the albino pirate. 'Is the hirsute pirate chap meant to be a metaphor for something?'

'I think he's possibly meant to be a goblin king. I've lost track a bit,' said the albino pirate.

Pretty soon Marx, Jennifer and the Captain could go no further. They'd reached the rim of the replica volcano's crater. The magma looked a lot like fondue bubbling away, and the Pirate Captain couldn't help but wish he was back on the boat, dipping things in melted cheese.

'Of course,' he said, 'what most people fail to realise is that it's actually the pyroclastic flow that's the really dangerous thing during an eruption rather than the rivers of red-hot lava.'

'You do seem to know a lot about volcanoes, Pirate Captain,' said Jennifer.

'Oh, I'm just a layman, to be honest,' said the Captain modestly. 'I went on a tour of Pompeii that one time.'

'Did you learn anything that might help us in our predicament?' asked Marx.

'The most important lesson I took away from the place is that if you're about to die from a volcano, then it's really vital to strike a heroic sort of pose. I don't want to be preserved for eternity cowering with my head between my legs like those Roman lubbers.'

'That's not much help.'

'No. Sorry. Well then, I suppose we could try plugging it.'

'With what?'

The Captain looked the hairy communist up and down. 'What would you say your physical dimensions are?'

'Captain!'

'I was only asking,' said the Pirate Captain defensively, deciding that Marx probably wouldn't be big enough anyhow. He looked about, at a loss. 'Pish. Where's a prize ham when you need one?'

'I fear it is the end for us,' wailed Marx as the bears inched closer. 'Is this the way you saw yourself going, Pirate Captain?'

'In fact,' said the Captain grumpily, 'it's pretty much the exact situation I usually try to cheer myself up with when I'm in a bit of a fix. "At least you're not about to be eaten by bears and/or fall into a replica volcano," I tell myself. So now I've got to come up with an even worse scenario, which is a nuisance.'

'It seems such a pity that two great minds should finish in such a way,' said Marx bitterly, teetering on the edge.

The Pirate Captain tugged at one of his bushy eyebrows as he tried to remember something. 'I seem to recall reading somewhere that in this sort of situation you're meant to make yourself look as big as possible.'

'Really? Not a fan of big things, bears?'

'Apparently not. I'll climb on your shoulders so it looks like we're just one big relatively hairy creature. Jennifer, you hide behind us, and do your best not to menstruate.'

'Why do I have to be the bottom half of the creature?' moaned Marx.

'Because I make a much better head,' said the Captain. 'I roar like a lion. It said so in the newspaper. Also I'm good at doing claw shapes with my hands, see?' The Captain did some claw shapes, and Marx reluctantly let him climb up onto his shoulders. They both fluffed out their beards to try to add to their fearsomeness.

'Raaargh!' said Marx.

'You can't go "Raaargh",' said the Captain. 'That just makes it look like our belly is growling.'

'Sorry,' said Marx.

'Those bears are going to eat the Pirate Captain and Jennifer,' said the pirate in green.

'Don't ruin the ending! You're always doing that,' said the pirate with a hook for a hand, looking cross. 'Just because you've seen this opera before doesn't mean we all have.'

Several of the crew leapt to their feet, ready to rush on the stage, but the pirate with a scarf held them back.

'If we just run up there,' he pointed out, trying not to sound bossy, 'we'll be eaten by the bears as well.'

'Oh dear,' said the albino pirate, sitting back down again. 'I don't like the sound of that.'

'Yes, you see this is why it pays to think plans through past the very first bit. Really that's what distinguishes "a plan" from "running about in a flap".'

The pirate with a scarf looked thoughtful for a moment, and then a wily look crept across his pleasingly rugged features.

'Captain!' he shouted.

'Hello there, number two,' the Pirate Captain called back, still making claw shapes at a bear. 'Fancy seeing you here! I've got all sorts to tell you, but unfortunately I'm a bit tied up at the moment.' He nodded at the bears.

'The pomade, Captain! The bear-grease pomade!'

'Oh, for goodness' sakes, I have got a few rather more pressing concerns,' grumbled the Captain. 'But if you insist.' He cleared his throat and waved at the audience.

'Perkins' Gentlemen's Pomade
Gives me flexible style.
Even when menaced by bears and a volcano,
I can still make ladies smile.'

Then he got Marx, straining under his weight a bit now, to do a little jig. The bears and the audience looked baffled.

'No, Captain,' shouted the pirate with a scarf, as patiently as he could. 'Try putting the pomade in your hair. It will make you smell like a bear.'

The pirate with a scarf then got the other pirates to take out their tins of pomade and made sure they all covered themselves with as much of the gloopy bear grease as possible. It looked a bit like ectoplasm, and some of the pirates started doing ghost impressions at each other, but then they remembered that they were at the climax of an adventure, so they stopped messing about and bounded on to the stage.

'Grrrr! I like eating picnic baskets,' said the pirate with rickets.

'And I'm a polar bear,' said the albino pirate. 'From the North Pole.'[31]

The bears sniffed at the pirates, then seemed to lose interest, and they wandered off to chew the scenery.

'It's working! They think we're greasy fellow bears,'

---

31. Polar bear liver contains so much vitamin A that it can be fatal if eaten by a human. Not that you should be eating polar bears anyhow.

said Engels, sprinting up the side of the volcano and giving Marx a welcoming hug.

'Everyone be careful not to look too attractive, especially you,' said the pirate with a scarf to the pirate with bedroom eyes, 'just in case the bears should mistake you for a potential mate. If we learnt one thing from our last adventure, it's that creatures' sexual appetites are best kept in check, or it leads to all sorts of problems.'

But before the pirates could begin to celebrate, or even just have a rest, there was a roar and an angry belch of black smoke and the colossal tin Nietzsche clumped onto the stage.

'Now who on earth is this?' said the Crowned Head of Portugal. 'These operas really are very difficult to follow.'

'I think he's Thor, who I believe is the god of hammering things,' said the Crowned Head of Bulgaria, studying his programme. 'Though it could also be a rock giant.'

A couple of the pirates looked momentarily triumphant and pulled told-you-so faces at their captain, because this proved that they really hadn't been exaggerating back in London. But then it dawned on them that being proved right about the existence of gigantic metal monsters is one of the worst things you can be proved right about, certainly nowhere near as good as being proved right about, say, having a magic hat or being a fantastic kisser or something like that. But those members of the crew who managed not to faint on the spot charged dutifully towards the mechanical man, waggling their cutlasses and bellowing deliberately hurtful nautical oaths.

'That's it, lads,' said the Pirate Captain encouragingly, as a few of the less important crew got squashed under one of Nietzsche's enormous tin feet. 'He can crush your bones, but he can't crush your indomitable spirit. Obviously, I'd love to help, but these futile sacrifices look like quite a lot of effort. And we can't risk me getting all sweaty. Because when you think about it, sweat is basically just hot water. And what happens when you put something in hot water? It shrinks. Which would be a disaster. What would you do with a shrunken captain?'

The pirates thought this was the opening line to a new shanty and began to sing, but another swipe of the colossal tin Nietzsche's arm sent most of them tumbling like skittles, though not quite enough fell down for any of the watching crowned heads to shout 'Strike!'

'Oh dear,' said the Pirate Captain. 'The tide appears to have turned. Which is a nautical way of saying that things have changed for the worse.'

He hopefully lobbed one of the empty tins of pomade at Nietzsche, but it just bounced off.

'Bother. We had exactly this difficulty in our adventure with Ned Kelly. It's his indestructible skin that's the problem.'

'I believe there may be one thing sharp enough to cut through his metal hide,' said Marx.

The Pirate Captain tried to think of sharp things. 'A crow's beak?'

'Sharper than a crow's beak, Captain.'

'A crow's beak made out of diamonds? Can you get those?'

'No.' Marx pulled out the slightly battered copy of the Pirate Captain's *Wit and Wisdom*. 'I was referring to your razor-sharp intellect.'

There was a bit of a pause. 'You're saying,' said the pirate in red, who was doing his best to hide behind the orchestra, 'that the Pirate Captain should *philosophise* a way out of the situation? Our same captain who, let's not forget, only last week was wondering out loud about whether eggs were a type of fruit?'

'Exactly!' cried Marx. 'A battle of wits. It will be like one of those Socratic dialogues from ancient times.'

'Except I don't remember any dialogue where Plato was trying to talk Socrates out of a diabolical plan for world domination,' pointed out Engels.

Nietzsche clumped heavily across the stage towards them, casting a monstrous shadow as he went. The Pirate Captain looked at the mechanical man's terrifying legs. He looked at his terrifying arms. He looked at his impassive metal face. And it occurred to him that if he had realised that the life of a philosopher boiled down to an endless series of perils, he might not have been quite so keen to take it up as a hobby.

'I can't help but think,' said the Pirate Captain, 'that possibly my abilities as a darling of the intellectual world have been a bit exaggerated.'

'Nonsense, Pirate Captain,' said Marx, fixing him with a serious stare. 'You, sir, are one of this era's great minds.'

'Oh well, when you put it like that.' The Captain cleared his throat. Nietzsche loomed menacingly over him. 'Excuse me, Clanky,' said the Pirate Captain. 'Can I call you Clanky?'

'I would rather you didn't,' said Nietzsche.

'Clanky, I'd like to try something out: It's what us philosopher types call a "thought experiment".'

The mechanical man stopped for a moment. 'What kind of thought experiment?'

'Well, stop me if I'm barking up the wrong tree, but I'm assuming this whole philosophical enterprise' – he gestured at the volcano, and the bears and the oblivious crowned heads – 'is something to do with trying to impress girls?'

'What makes you think that?' said Nietzsche. He sounded like he would have been blushing, if tin could blush, which obviously it can't.[32]

---

32. Though, due to its crystalline structure, tin can emit a high-pitched squeak when you bend it, known as 'tin cry'.

'Oh, you know.' The Pirate Captain shrugged. 'There's the fixation with goblins and magic rings and that kind of thing, which is always a clue that there may be social issues involved. But more importantly, it's my firm belief that trying to impress women is ninety-nine per cent of the motivation for anything ever. Including, but not limited to, philosophising. For instance, you've got Marx here, with his "don't let rich people turn orphans into glue" nonsense. That's obviously to make him look like good caring-husband material. Or take Plato,' the Captain went on, getting into his stride now, 'with the whole "platonic love" thing, which anyone can see was just to get some nice Greek girl not to feel too threatened by him before he moved in on her with that "oh, I've gone and spilt wine on your toga" trick. And Kant, he's another one, banging on about metaphysics, because it's floaty and a bit nebulous, like how ponies are.'

'It's an interesting theory,' agreed Nietzsche grudgingly.

'So what I propose is this: we have an actual lady here.' The Pirate Captain pointed at Jennifer, who waved. 'And what we do is play out a little scenario where you pretend you've just met her and explain your philosophy. Then we see how much she wants to be your girlfriend. Is that all right with you, Jennifer?'

'No problem,' said Jennifer.

'And if it turns out you're right, Clanky, then I promise you won't hear another peep out of any of us. I'll even help you feed me to the bears by showing off my thighs, which can only be described as succulent looking. Well?'

'Oh, go on then,' said Nietsche.

'Right. So this is Jennifer. You've just met her in the park while feeding the ducks. You have to use your imagination. What are you going to say?'

'Erm . . . Hello, Jennifer.'

'Hello, Nietzsche.'

'These ducks are nice, aren't they?'

'Yes, they are. Lovely.'

'So, um, what music are you into?'

'I like a bit of everything, really,' said Jennifer.

'I hate almost all music, especially anything that's popular. I'm really into, you know, opera and stuff. You've probably never heard of most of it.'

'Probably not,' said Jennifer. 'I don't really follow music that closely. What brings you to the park today?'

'I'm here to think about things. I'm a philosopher.'

'Oh, really? How interesting. What's your philosophy?'

'I call it "Fascism". It's quite radical.'

'Is it something to do with faces?'

'Not exactly, although we fascists do prefer to see faces with moustaches on them, topped with a neat side parting.'

'I see.' Jennifer threw some imaginary bread to an imaginary duck.

'Yes – and you know how most philosophers write everything down in big boring books? Well, I don't do that. In fact, I prefer *burning* books to reading them.'

'That's a bit drastic,' said Jennifer; 'you can learn some great things from books.'

'Perhaps, but it's my belief that people are basically stupid and any sort of knowledge at all will cause more harm than good.'

'So what are your main ideas?'

Aphorisms are my big thing.'

'Aphorisms?'

'Sayings, stuff like "If a woman possesses manly virtues, one should run away from her; and if she does not possess them, she runs away from herself".'

'OK. But that's not really proper philosophising, is it? It's more like what you'd find in a greetings card.'

'I also want more atrocities and stiffer hats.'

'It's got a bit cold in the park,' said Jennifer. 'I probably ought to be off.'

'That's the cold wind of destiny sweeping Europe, bringing about a glorious fascist future.'[33]

There was an awkward pause, broken only by the albino pirate doing a duck impression and quacking for more bread. Eventually, Nietzsche spoke up again. 'So

---

33. Believe it or not, the *Daily Mail* wasn't always the enlightened bastion of reasoned debate that it is today. In 1924 the paper even printed an article about Oswald Mosley's blackshirts entitled 'Hurrah for Fascists!'.

will you go out with me? You have reasonable childbearing hips for breeding a healthy brood of fascist babies.'

'And . . . break,' said the Pirate Captain. 'Well then, Jennifer, what do you think? Should I be buying a new wedding hat?'

'I'm afraid not, Pirate Captain. What Nietzsche has forgotten is that we women don't tend to go in for authoritarian dogma. We prefer someone who is good company, can anticipate our feelings and make us laugh from time to time.'

'And you, Clanky? How do you think that went?'

For a moment there was no reply. Marx, Engels and all the pirates held their breath.

'It's . . . erm . . . I realise now that what looked good on paper feels a bit silly when you say it out loud.'[34]

'You see? I'm not known for my metaphors, but if you ask me, this philosophy of yours would be like . . .' The Captain paused, and thought for a moment. '. . . like a dirty great boot stamping on the face of humanity for ever. And have you ever tried to make out with a pretty girl whilst a huge boot stamps on the pair of you for ever? It's not so easy.'

The big metal philosopher let out a sad little puff of steam. Then there was a hissing sound as a door in his chest popped open, and a pale young man with a droop-

---

34. In 1882 Nietzsche arranged for a photograph with his friend Paul Ree, pretending to be oxen pulling a cart containing Lou Salome, who is whipping them. This bizarre attempt at romance failed, as Nietzsche later proposed to Salome and was turned down.

ing moustache clambered out from the mess of levers and wires and cams and spindles in which he had been sat. He climbed down from his contraption and sheepishly dusted a bit of oil from his coat.

'I think I've made a terrible mistake,' he said sadly.

'It's all right,' said the Pirate Captain. 'You're just a kid really. We all try to be slightly outrageous when we're your age. I got my first tattoo about that time.' He rolled up his sleeve and indicated a faded bluish picture of an angry adolescent pirate saying 'Parents just don't understand' on his left arm. 'I only did it to annoy them. With the benefit of hindsight I can appreciate that it's quite a naïve sentiment.'

'I'm sorry about your pirates,' said Nietzsche, looking at the bits of squashed pirate that were littered across the stage. 'And the almost-having-you-eaten-by-angry-bears thing. You must think the worst of me.'

'Aarrrr. Don't worry,' said the Captain. 'If I've learnt one thing as a pirate, it's that wherever you go, from Chesterfield to Matlock, there are only two kinds of diabolical villain: there's the misunderstood kind who are doing it for the attention, and then there's the evil-to-the-core kind. Actually, I'm forgetting zombies. There are three kinds of villain: misunderstood ones who are doing it for the attention, evil-to-the-core types and zombies. And inscrutable foreigners as well. Four types—'

'Captain,' said Marx.

'Yes, sorry. Anyway, I look at you' – the Captain patted

Nietzsche on his head – 'and I can tell you're one of the misunderstood types.'

'I suppose I am a little misunderstood,' said Nietzsche, sounding rueful. 'It's just girls. The truth is, they terrify me.'

'Of course they do. Everyone's scared of girls. Even other girls.'

'Even you?'

'Oh, yes. Even someone as dashing and debonair as myself has relationship difficulties.' The Pirate Captain took his wallet from his pocket and pulled out a battered photograph.

'There. That's the woman in my life,' he said wistfully.

'This is a picture of the sea,' said Nietzsche.

'Yes, and between you and me she's a nightmare. Wobbly. All over the place. Always making me ill.' The Pirate Captain grinned. 'But I love her nonetheless.'

Thirteen

MURDER AMONGST
THE MOLLUSCS

M arx, Engels and Nietzsche had all come down to
the banks of the Seine to see the pirates off.

'I'm sorry you won't reconsider things,' said Marx,
warmly clasping the Captain's hand. 'You still have so
much to offer the world of philosophical thought.'

'That's true,' said the Pirate Captain. 'But the trouble
with this philosophy lark is that it involves a lot of intro-
spection. And the thing I'm probably proudest of is my
near total lack of self-awareness. It's what makes me the
man I am.'

'Well, look after yourself. Now that this little scally-
wag' – Marx gave Nietzsche a friendly wink – 'isn't caus-
ing us mischief, I feel it is only a matter of time before

our reputation is restored and Communism really takes off. Especially now I've adopted some of your more pork-orientated ideas.'

'It's all in the type of glaze you use,' said the Captain. 'I honestly can't emphasise that enough.'

'And we'd like to give you this, as a going-away present,' said Engels, handing him a painting. It showed the Pirate Captain looking burly and heroic, stood atop a big red shooting star. The rosy-cheeked peasant girl who seemed to feature in a lot of the communists' paintings was holding on to his leg adoringly.

'Aaarrrr,' said the Pirate Captain, 'I'm touched. It will go very well with my new giant novelty candle.' He nodded towards where a couple of pirates were hefting the wax Queen Victoria onboard the boat. Then he turned towards Nietzsche. 'So then, young man. You'll remember what I've taught you?'

'Yes, Pirate Captain,' replied Nietzsche, looking serious. 'Aloof – funny – deep. Always in that order.'

'I'm sure the right girl will come along soon,' said Jennifer. She kissed Nietzsche on the cheek, and he turned a bright shade of red, but grinned from ear to ear.

'They're going to kick themselves when they realise that in saving all those crowned heads, they've put back the revolution by about fifty years,' said the pirate with a scarf as the boat slowly pulled out from the jetty.

'Yes, I think that's what they call the ultimate irony,' said the Pirate Captain. 'Or possibly the penultimate irony. Because in many ways the ultimate irony is the fact that philosophy has lost us our sponsorship deal. It turns out that Perkins' Pomades don't want to be associated with' – he read from the letter they had received that morning, – '"the kind of pirate who ends an adventure with reasoned and sensitive debate rather than multiple eviscerations and/or explosions". Still, nothing ventured, nothing gained, or whatever the appropriate expression is in this instance.'

They turned away from watching Paris fade into the distance and looked instead at the pirates who were playing with the various bits of Nietzsche's gigantic tin suit, which they had brought onboard the boat as a souvenir. At the moment what appeared to be Nietzsche's hand with some stripy pirate legs coming out of the bottom of it was running about trying to catch Nietzsche's elbow, which was getting tangled up in the rigging.

The Captain sighed. 'In a way, don't we all build up an impregnable metal suit around ourselves?' he said wisely. 'Except the suit is made of emotions and neuroses and things, instead of tin, so you can't see it. And it doesn't have light bulbs for eyes. And it's not steam-powered.'

'That's very true,' said the pirate with a scarf, who didn't have the faintest clue what the Pirate Captain was going on about.

And with that, the pirates went downstairs to do some shantying.

Appendix: *The Wit and Wisdom of the Pirate Captain* – a Major Philosophical Work

The Fable of the Pig and the Rooster

In the olden days there was a pig and a rooster, but the rooster was quite arrogant. It was this that led to his inevitable downfall.

On the Question of Ethics

Most people have a 'moral compass' – an internal sense that tells them whether any given act is the correct one to do. If, say, someone asked you to run over a load of vicars with a train, you'd have a think, check your moral compass and decide whether or not to do it. You'd need to get hold of a train, of course, but the argument still works.

I've taken this one step further – I'm not really one for abstract concepts, because if you think about them for too long your forehead starts to ache from all the frowning. So what I recommend is that you make a real moral compass out of a paper plate. Just get a pen and draw on some 'compass points' – for example, mine has 'Right', 'Wrong', 'Wrong but feels right', 'Will anybody find out?' and 'Who can say?' In the middle, make a little pointer and fix it with a split pin – you can get these from most good stationers. Then when you face a decision, spin the moral compass and see what your conscience tells you.

On the Matter of Love

If you're off to fight in a battle, snap a ship's biscuit in half and give your girlfriend the other half. When you meet again, they will match – like two halves of a single soul! Hopefully, this will stop her sleeping with other men.

On the Question of Knowledge

Occasionally, you meet a stupid person who tells you something ridiculous – like he's bought your book and he can't help thinking he could have written it better himself. You have to ask him how he knows this and he can rarely answer you – especially when you've smashed a vase on his face. But it's an interesting question. How can we ever say what we know and don't know? What does it mean to say, 'I *know* that egg is hard-boiled' or 'I *know* that there's a pig hidden under that duvet, and I'm not going to tell you scurvy rotters about keeping pigs in your cabins again'?

In my experience, the best way to find out if you really know something is to ask your second-in-command. Second-in-commands remember all kinds of things that you'll have forgotten. If you don't have a second-in-command, then I can't help you.

On the Question of Gravy Stains

It is my opinion that the best way to get gravy stains out of cotton or wool is to soak the fabric in vinegar for half an hour and then rinse thoroughly with cold water. If this doesn't work, try burning the gravy off with a match or getting a hungry dog to lick it off.

On the Matter of Kids

There is nothing funnier than a child saying something either wise beyond his years or charmingly naïve.

On the Existence of God

On the face of it, this seems patently absurd. The modern forward-facing pirate uses reason and logic, and isn't about to accept the existence of a deity without any proof.

Ah! But if there was a god, that might be exactly how he wants it. He might want to be able to move amongst his creations incognito. To do this, he'd need to choose an occupation that enabled him to travel around easily, something like a door-to-door salesman, or a hobo, or even a *pirate*. He wouldn't want to show off his all-encompassing knowledge, so he'd probably *deliberately get stuff wrong*, like, for example, if he was being asked to explain what various nautical terms meant. Also, bear in mind that in all the paintings you see of God he has a *great big beard*. Anyhow, I've already said too much.

On the Matter of Plants

Don't throw away empty yoghurt pots – they make excellent pots for small plants.

On the Question of Classification

You can divide the animal kingdom into five different classes:

Animals: identifiable by their characteristic four legs, animals are probably the most famous creatures available. Meat comes from here.

Sea creatures: includes sharks, crocodiles, whales, barnacles and other fish. Distinguished from animals by being slimy and more suited to parsley sauce.

Sea monsters: the most fearsome class, sea monsters vary widely. The common theme is that when you tell people about them, they assume you are lying. A fascinating fact: zombies are technically in this category, although none of them live in the sea!

Birds: anything with wings. Birds evolved when the earth was still covered in lava and therefore too hot to walk around on.

Fungus: mushrooms, toadstools and athlete's foot. If you go for a walk in the woods and see a fungus, why not eat it? It's a proven scientific fact that a creature that doesn't move can't hurt you.

Any creatures that don't fit these classes are the exceptions that prove the rule.

On Life in General

Life is like a big shanty. Everything will be fine so long as everyone sings in harmony. But if someone plays a duff note on the accordion or tries to break-dance at a sensitive bit, then there will be all sorts of trouble, mark my words.

On Discipline Running a Pirate Boat

An old sock and a couple of shells can be used to create a sock puppet that acts as a useful teaching aid when dealing with the slower pirates on your crew. You can name your sock puppet anything you like, but I'd recommend either 'Socky' or 'Lord Socklington'.

On Delicious Fudge Brownies

6 oz rich dark chocolate (minimum 60% cocoa solids)
9 oz softened butter
5 big eggs
1 lb caster sugar
Drop of vanilla extract
4½ oz plain flour
2 oz cocoa powder
Some chopped walnuts

Melt butter and sugar together in a pan, remove from heat and beat in remaining ingredients. Put the whole lot in a roasting tin lined with greased tracing paper and stick in the oven for forty minutes. Remove from oven and leave to cool on a wire rack.

If any of your pirate crew try and pinch one before they're cooled, playfully smack them on the back of the hand with a wooden spoon and say, 'Naughty! Oh no, you don't!'

A Note on the Type

This book is set in Golombek Bold. Developed in the 1950s by Sergei Golombek as a means of smuggling secrets out of Stalinist Russia, each full stop is really a microdot containing the blueprints of reactor cores, submarines and missile silos. And hidden inside the loop of the letter 'g' is a map showing the true location of where Lenin's brain is kept frozen inside a special refrigerated box!

PERKINS GENTLEMEN'S POMADE

BEAR GREASE

MONTMARTR

OPERA

ARC DE TRIOMPHE

R. SEINE

MOULIN ROUGE

TOUR EIFFEL

Hello Lubbers!

If you ever find yourself in Paris, chances are it won't be because you're having an exciting adventure with communists. More likely you'll be trying to get someone into bed. So here are a few ROMANTIC PICK-UP LINES to tell your beloved.

"Did you know that the Eiffel Tower has 2·5 million rivets? That's a lot of rivets!"

"In 1349 as many as 800 Parisians died of the black plague every single day!"

"In Godzilla Destroy All Monsters Gerodauius knocks down the Arc de Triomphe!"

Saying any of these is pretty much guaranteed to get you to third base.

Your's *The Pirate Captain*